# EARTH ALIENS

# Demons in the North

S.E. Wendel

**E**

EPIC
Press

Demons in the North
Earth Aliens: Book #2

Written by S.E. Wendel

Copyright © 2016 by Abdo Consulting Group, Inc.

Published by EPIC Press™
PO Box 398166
Minneapolis, MN 55439

Cover design by Dorothy Toth
Images for cover art obtained from iStockPhoto.com
Edited by Clete Barrett Smith

Library of Congress Cataloging-in-Publication Data

Wendel, S.E.
Demons in the north / S.E. Wendel.
p. cm. — (Earth aliens ; #2)
Summary: After seven brutal years aboard starships, the humans have landed on
their new home planet, Terra Nova, and it isn't the paradise they had hoped. The
Earth aliens begin to put roots down, however the shocking realization is becoming
increasingly clearer, that they may not be alone.
ISBN 978-1-68076-023-1 (hardcover)
1. Aliens—Fiction. 2. Human-alien encounters—Fiction. 3. Extraterrestrial
beings—Fiction. 4. Science fiction. 5. Young adult fiction. I. Title.
[Fic]—dc23
2015935811

EPIC
Press

EPICPRESS.COM

*To Kim, who could write her own book about the madness of living with an author*

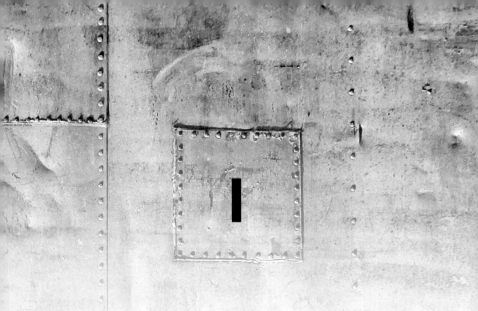

**E**lena Ames drummed her fingers along the thick barrel of her gun. It was heavy, heavier than the practice guns she was used to. She rolled her shoulders, trying to tamp down her nerves a little. She had been training seven years for this.

She had left Earth a little girl. Earth was dying—actually was probably dead by now. They had left it to die, 40,000 pioneers lucky enough to colonize what everyone hoped would be a new beginning. Now they were home, and she wasn't little anymore.

The landing had gone smoothly enough, no

crashes or malfunctions. A blessing after a bleak, hard life aboard ship. They had lost one starship along the way, but no one talked about that.

She waited quietly with the rest of her squadron in a hangar bay. There were six teams working to get some cruisers running, the armored vehicles serving as a sort of vanguard for the squad headed out.

*Out.* The word had a sort of electricity about it. It made the tips of Elena's fingers tingle.

They had been cooped up on the starships for three days while preliminary tests were run. It was better than anyone could have imagined. The initial hypotheses about the atmosphere had been correct—it was similar to Earth's, but without all the pollution. Ground samples came back positive: seeds brought light-years from Earth would grow on Terra Nova.

"Right then. Listen up!" came a sharp voice.

Everyone went rigid, standing straight and saluting General Hammond as she walked in. The military leader of the expedition, the general had overseen them all the past seven years. She was tough. She was demanding. But they had faith she would keep them alive.

All of them, that was, except Elena. Life had been hard aboard ship, and the general hadn't made it any easier. There had been quiet talk, but talk nonetheless about it being the general's fault that one of the starships failed and exploded mid-flight. She had pushed it too hard. The general pushed everything too hard—why, Elena couldn't guess.

The general put her hands behind her back, giving each soldier a stony stare. She was a no-nonsense leader, and Elena couldn't think of an instance when she had seen the general with anything other than a scowl. Hammond gave her orders sharply and expected absolute obedience. She didn't take criticism. The fact that it had gotten around that she hadn't been the first choice to lead the expedition no doubt irked her.

"I want to see focus out there. I know it's been a long time coming. You're going to be the first to step foot on our new home, but first we must create a perimeter and secure the immediate area. Is that understood?"

"Yes, ma'am!"

"I don't want to see any daydreaming. Anyone I see getting an imagination gets sent straight back to the ship. Is that understood?"

"Yes, ma'am!"

She nodded. "Out you go, then."

There was the sound of grinding metal, and suddenly a bright shaft of light pierced the hangar. It was blinding and foreign and wonderful.

Sunlight on Earth had been dangerous. All children knew to stay out of it as much as possible. Elena herself had proof of that: a wide pockmark on her right arm where they had taken the melanoma out when she was eight.

But this sunlight was different. As the door rose

up, letting the light of two suns in, she felt warm. It touched her gently.

The cruisers groaned, sleepy after their long journey. The first, then a second, headed down the ramp and onto the ground outside. The call went out, and the squad began moving too.

Elena had to stop her knees from quaking. As she walked down the ramp, she forgot the general's warning about inattention. There was just too much to see.

The air was crisp, clean, spicy with the smell of upturned earth. The cold ground crunched a little beneath her feet, the dirt a rich red-brown. She looked up to see a sky so blue it almost hurt to look at. Wispy silver clouds were meandering towards the horizon.

She almost jumped at an elbow to her ribs.

She looked left, scowling, expecting to see Oscar Livermore, her rival apprentice. Instead she found Sergeant Rhiannon White, her mentor during the long trip.

Sgt. White was grinning, though exasperated. "Eyes up, soldier."

Elena nodded, falling into step behind her. She couldn't bear getting sent back to the ship now. She would never go inside ever again.

The squad fanned out across the wide crater the ship had made upon landing. Thrusters had spared them from a bumpy landing, but they had done a number on the landscape nonetheless.

Some soldiers considered every step, their guns at the ready. Others had their head on a swivel, trying to take everything in. They all moved towards the crest of the crater, anxious to see more.

Elena couldn't get over how quiet it was. Not like on the ship when walking down an empty corridor. This was peaceful. A light breeze rustled the trees up ahead. The sky was enormous, but not forlorn like the empty black of space. It looked like pictures of Earth back before technology, before the beginning of the end.

She followed the sergeant up the slope, filled

her lungs with the strong scent of dirt. She took a handful of it, let it fall in little clumps between her fingers. Her heart swelled at feeling the dirt. There was life in it, unlike the arid sand of Earth.

She almost ran into Sgt. White at the top. Dodging quickly to the left, she put a foot on the crest and heaved herself up to stand beside the sergeant. She saw what the hold-up was.

Before them the land stretched out for miles and miles. The starships had landed amongst rolling hills populated by wide, thick trees. They weren't like Earth trees—they were bigger, taller, their leaves slick and wide and their bark almost red.

To the immediate south the foothills quickly flattened out into a narrow valley, the peaks of more hills just visible against the horizon line. The valley was golden, colored by what looked like some sort of grass, and tapered off to the east.

To the north the hills scaled upwards into snow-capped mountains. Elena shivered just looking

at them, but was enthralled at the idea of snow. Powdery frozen water had become as good as myth back on Earth.

It was what was along the southern horizon, however, that drew the most attention. At the far side of the golden valley were small plumes of smoke.

A native village lay just out of sight.

---

Outside was bright. Rhys O'Callahan squinted, his vision still blurry from recently coming out of cryogenic sleep. The brightness hurt his sore eyes, but he sure as hell wasn't going back.

"Easy now," said Hugh, his twin brother.

Well, twin wasn't exactly right anymore. Whereas Rhys had been put to cryogenic sleep for seven years, Hugh had been selected to be an apprentice, getting to stay awake for the journey.

Now Hugh was almost nineteen while Rhys was still eleven.

"I'm fine," Rhys said, pushing Hugh's hand away.

Seven years and his brother hadn't changed much. He was taller, his voice was deeper, and he had stubble that made his chin prickly. But he was Hugh, always the worrier. What unnerved Rhys about it was seeing what he himself would look like when he grew up. Honestly he didn't like their nose, too pointy.

Hugh moved off a little but continued to hover.

Rhys tried to ignore him, wholly interested in the feel of fresh dirt beneath his feet. It had been torture staying aboard a whole week with the other sleepers. One of Hugh's friends, Elena, had gotten to go out with the military to set up a perimeter, and now that it was done, all the civilians could get their first glimpse of Terra Nova.

Putting his hands on his hips, Rhys took a deep breath, drinking in the fresh air.

"Can you believe it?" he said.

"No, not yet at least," said Hugh, his hands in his pockets. He grinned at the ground, kicking a clump of dirt with the toe of his boot. "It's just like you said."

Rhys peered at him, squinting a little to put him in focus.

Hugh's gaze was distant, his smile wistful. "It's green. And it's ours."

"And you said you wouldn't like green," said Rhys, punching Hugh in the arm. He was a little irritated at having to get on his toes to do so.

Grinning, the boys continued on with the flow of colonists to the top of the crater to look out at the surrounding landscape.

The uneven ground made each step an adventure, and soon Rhys was darting about, trying to find the quickest way to the top. He scrambled up the slope, his hands browned by the time he got there. Hugh hurried up behind him.

"Would you look at that."

The land stretched out seemingly forever in rolling hills of green and brown and red and gold. To the north the deep blue sky touched white peaks along a jagged horizon.

Something to the south caught Rhys's eye. He squinted.

"Maybe we should ask about getting you some glasses," said Hugh.

Rhys gave him a particularly sour expression.

"What's out there?" he asked, pointing to the south.

Hugh looked too. "It looks like . . . "

"What?" Rhys prodded Hugh's side.

"Smoke."

"Is there a fire?"

"We're closer than we should be . . . "

"Closer to what?"

"We should've landed further to the east."

"What're you talking about?"

Hugh continued muttering to himself, making Rhys aggravated. His lips pursed, he shoved at

Hugh. This accomplished little more than making Hugh take half a step to steady himself, only irritating Rhys more.

Finally Hugh looked down at him. His brows were drawn together. He looked about before squatting down.

Rhys's nose wrinkled.

"There're natives over there," Hugh said.

"Natives?" The word felt funny on his tongue. "What like aliens?"

"Sort of. There's intelligent life here other than us. That must be a village down there."

"What're they like?"

"We don't know yet."

He looked over his shoulder, making sure no one was listening. He put a big hand on Rhys's shoulder, which he tried to squirm out of, but Hugh held fast.

"Don't go talking about this, okay? It's not common knowledge yet."

"What's that mean?"

"The general will tell everyone soon. But for now it's a secret."

Rhys didn't like secrets—at least, he didn't like them being kept from him. He felt offended for the other sleepers. They had been told very little after waking, just that they had arrived safely and that their new lives would start soon. The only reason he knew about the lost fifth starship was because of Hugh.

That was another thing that hadn't changed; Hugh could never keep a secret, not from Rhys. They didn't have secrets. As he and Hugh began walking down into the trees, he wondered if that would still be the case. Hugh carried himself in a way Rhys couldn't describe—like his shoulders were weighed down. He didn't like not being able to name it.

They continued on into the trees, touching the land for themselves. As they walked, Rhys couldn't help letting his mind run rampant with ideas about the natives. He thought of all the alien species in old Earth movies and wondered if they would be like lizards, with long tongues, or perhaps tall and catlike. Perhaps they would be huge sentient blobs with no eyes, only a gaping mouth.

He grinned to himself as he thought about it. All options sounded interesting.

People were streaming out of their ships, heading for one of several stations set up that were passing out tents, several days' rations, and some other small necessities. They would be living in a tent city while the ships were deconstructed to be repurposed.

Hugh steered them away from the nearest station, where many sleepers were gathering, and instead headed for a further one. As they got closer, Rhys saw that those waiting for supplies here were uniformed.

"What's wrong with the one back there?" he asked.

"We're going to be stationed here," Hugh answered, getting in the back of the line.

"What's so great about here?"

"It'll eventually be the military's section of the residential quadrant."

"You're not in the military."

"No, but our department will be overseen by the military."

Rhys frowned. "*Our?*"

"Well, yeah. Didn't I tell you? I got you assigned to the engineering department, with Saranov and me."

"No, you didn't tell me."

Rhys crossed his arms and scowled. The last thing he wanted to do on their new planet was talk about nuts and bolts all day. Hugh had been making hints that he was going to get Rhys assigned with him to the engineers, always talking excitedly about getting to work together, but Rhys had hoped his less than enthusiastic attitude would have told his brother how he really felt about the situation. Apparently not.

"Well," said Hugh, beginning to pick at his thumb, "it'll be fine. You'll see."

"I don't want—"

Hugh shushed him with a wave of his hand and stepped up to the officer in charge. Hugh was given a large canvas square, a bag of steel rods, and a sack of other necessities. There was little room in his arms for the two blanket rolls the officer had left to give.

"Rhys."

Grabbing up the blankets, Rhys followed Hugh, trying not to pout.

They headed up along the east side of the crater with a line of others. They made for a small grotto. There was an officer standing at the mouth with a reader, a thin device that projected a screen.

"Serial?" he asked Hugh as they approached.

"Two-four-six-nine-eight," said Hugh.

The officer waited until a picture of Hugh popped up on his reader, then nodded his head. Sticking a thumb over his shoulder he said, "Pick a plot and set up camp. You'll be reporting for deconstruction at oh-seven-hundred tomorrow."

"Great, thanks."

Rhys lifted his foot to follow Hugh, stopped at the officer's hand suddenly in his face. He glowered up at the man.

"What?"

"You're pretty young for an apprentice. Serial?"

Rhys opened his mouth.

"Two-four-six-nine-seven," Hugh said quickly. "Sorry, he's with me. Reassignment."

The officer nodded again. "Right, here it is. Off you go."

Shouldering the blankets, Rhys stalked behind Hugh. He glared at the back of his brother's head, annoyed at having to crane his neck to do so.

Hugh picked a spot that was close to an enormous tree.

"This'll be good right? Plenty of shade."

Rhys shrugged.

He barely helped put up the tent, leaving Hugh to thread the steel rods and stringing lines all by himself. Rhys held what he was asked to hold, stood where he was asked to stand, the whole while fuming. Where did Hugh come off answering for him? *He* was the older twin. *He* knew what to do, where to go, what to say. At least, he had.

"There!" said Hugh, wiping off his brow and taking a step back to survey his work. "How's that?"

Rhys barely looked at the perfectly pitched tent.

"I don't want to be an engineer."

**2**

The Red Hall rang with the echoes of shouting voices, everyone trying to say their peace all at once. Zeneba, the new leader, or *mara*, of the Charneki, rubbed her temples.

Before her stood the many members of her council, most of them turquoise-robed Elders. Her tutors for the past cycles, many had transitioned into positions on her council, though there was one notable difference now that she was *mara*.

"This will accomplish nothing," said Elder Zhora, her new head councilor.

His sightless eyes, trained on the roar of noise,

were shadowed by a deep frown. He had been troubled of late. They all were.

Zeneba was tired. She had slept very little. Every piece of news they got about the stars that had landed in the north was another trouble. Messengers from the tundra had rushed to her, claiming that the stars were in fact buildings of some sort, vast, silver, and bearing some kind of beings.

She rubbed her closed eyes with one of her two long fingers and her thumb. She held her other hand up.

At first nothing happened, then a heavy *clank* made the floor tremble. She looked up to meet the new silence the Head of her Guard had created with his heavy spear. She gave Yaro an appreciative nod before turning back to her council.

"Wise Ones," she began in the formal accent of the capital, "we are blind to the problem before us. Yet we must act, and quickly. Now, I want to hear what you would advise me to do. One at a time."

Some looked rather embarrassed as all the

members drew closer to the dais where the royal seat stood, carved from the topmost red stones of their mountain-city.

Elder Vasya, the Charneki who had headed Zeneba's council during her minority, stepped forwards.

"We must act decisively, Golden One," he said.

There was grumbling behind him.

"To hesitate will only show weakness," he insisted. "Whatever these demons may be, they do not seem to be leaving. We must see that they do."

"Are we quite sure they are demons, then?" she asked.

Elder Vasya's lips twitched. "We do not know what they are. Or what they want."

"Which is why we must study them!" insisted Elder Jeska. He pushed his way to the front of the crowd. "How do we know if we can force them to leave? Perhaps we cannot. In such a case, there may be something we can offer them, something—"

"You wish to *appease* these demons?" Elder Vasya spat.

"I seek only a diplomatic solution. I do not have your warmongering tastes, Vasya."

"Approaching them will solve nothing!" Elder Plia cried, coming to the front, too. "We must secure the people, see to our defenses, and wait for them to leave."

"Are you so sure they will?" Elder Vasya scoffed.

"To attack them would be madness!"

This only renewed the shouting, and Zeneba found her head aching again.

"You must forgive them," said Elder Zhora, patting her narrow shoulder. "They are scared."

"You trained me for this," she told him, "prepared me for their coming. Now they're here and I don't know what to do."

Her head sank into her hands, and her swirls of iridescent skin, the pattern different for every Charneki, fell into a deep blue. As *mara*, she had been trained long hours to control the iridescence, the *harn-da*, yet she did not care to even try right then. She was too tired.

"Find the middle ground. They are all right, though they speak opposites. You must see a way between them."

Wiping at her eyes, Zeneba dared look back out at her council. Few of them were looking at her, engrossed in the heated debate. The council was beginning to break into factions.

Zeneba nodded at Yaro again, and he seemed pleased to raise his spear and bring it back down with a ringing effect.

"This is getting us nowhere," Zeneba said once the council had quieted. She stole a glance at Elder Zhora before saying, "We must know more about these demons. Perhaps they can be persuaded to leave—" she held up a hand, silencing Elder Vasya, "—perhaps they have some weakness we can use. I do not wish to send any Charneki towards harm, but we cannot stay within our walls and do nothing."

"Golden One, please, what of my people? We haven't the strength to keep them at bay should they advance."

Chieftain Ura made his way to the front of the council as he spoke. A broad, powerful Charneki, he stood taller even than Yaro. Charneki were commonly slight, with narrow shoulders and hips. Their solid feet—usually the widest part of them—tapered up to slender calves and thighs. The Chieftain looked the part of a brave warlord.

Zeneba nodded, considering what Chieftain Ura said. His tundra region villages were the closest to the fallen stars.

"I would like to send a scouting party back with the Chieftain, to help make safe the tundra and study the demons. We will learn what we can. In the meantime, send out warnings to all the clans; tell them to be cautious and await further word." She told Chieftain Ura specifically, "My best warriors from my own Guard will accompany you back."

The Chieftain bowed low.

"And who will lead such a party?" asked Elder Vasya.

She had to suppress her smile when a name

popped into her head. Perhaps she could solve two problems at once.

Turning her head to Yaro, she said, "Can you bring me Ondra, please?"

Yaro's mouth was a narrow line as he nodded at a guard standing near the threshold of the Red Hall.

"Ondra is brave and able," she told Chieftain Ura, "and he will be at your disposal."

"Thank you, Golden One."

The noise grew again, but it sounded less hostile now. The Elders were most concerned with figuring out a list of things for the scouting party to look for and asking Chieftain Ura what supplies his people might need from the Capital. Yaro took the moment to move closer to Zeneba.

Only she could hear him say, "Forgive me, Golden One, but Ondra has only just passed the trials. He is untested."

Zeneba expected as much. Yaro disapproved of Ondra, her childhood friend, being admitted to the elite Guard. It had been at Zeneba's behest, not Ondra's own merit. Ondra had come almost two cycles ago, tall, strong, even a little dashing—though Zeneba would never admit it to him. Always fiery, he had become proud of his skills as a warrior, a pride that Yaro sought to replace with humility. That was proving more difficult than either he or Zeneba had thought, and she knew she wouldn't be making it easier for Yaro by giving Ondra this assignment. She did, however, believe that putting Ondra out into the world might help him realize the weight of Yaro's teachings.

She grinned up at Yaro. "This seems as good a test as any. And Chieftain Ura will be overseeing him."

"I know it is futile asking, but would you not rather send someone more experienced?"

"I must send someone I absolutely trust, so my only other alternative is to send you," she said, "and we both know I can't do that. I need you here."

She had to hide her amused grin watching the

thoughts cross over Yaro's eyes. He was proud and soldierly and certainly wouldn't admit to feeling hurt that he hadn't been given the honor of acting in the *mara*'s name. Yet she needed him here—she wasn't sure she could manage without him. He was her strength when she needed a little more than her own, and when holding council, it was comforting to know she had at least one friend standing beside her.

There was, of course, another reason. She didn't have to wait long for Yaro to arrive at it too. Having successfully kept a zealous Ondra, for the most part, away from Zeneba during his time in Karak, Yaro's lip twitched at the idea of leaving him unsupervised.

Yaro bowed. "Perhaps time away will do him good."

"My thoughts exactly."

Ondra didn't keep them waiting long. He wore a rather besmirched breastplate and was flushed, as if he had been summoned away from the practice grounds. His lithe body, while narrow, moved with a warrior's grace, and Zeneba had to smile watching Ondra, under Yaro's eye, attempt to walk slow and dignified towards her.

When he neared the seat, he bowed low. He almost opened his mouth to say something, but stopped when his eyes flicked to Yaro.

"Ondra," she said, the awkwardness of addressing him so formally almost making her giggle, "I have a task for you."

He bowed again. "Name it, Golden One."

"You will lead an outfit and accompany Chieftain Ura back to the tundra. There you will aid him with whatever he sees fit for the defense of his villages. When this is done, your party will observe these demons and learn what you can."

Ondra smiled broadly, flushing gold. "It will be done!"

Zeneba held out her hand, and Ondra approached the seat enthusiastically to take it.

Out of the corner of her eye she could see Yaro grimacing.

Once he had taken her hand she said, "Mark me, you are not to engage the demons. You are to seek knowledge, not bloodshed."

He nodded. "I understand."

"Go then, and may Nahara and Undin smile upon you."

He bowed a grateful head, touching the back of her hand with his forehead.

She gripped his hand tight, not letting him step back.

"Here's your chance," she whispered to him. "Don't fail me."

He straightened, smiling. "I wouldn't dream of it."

———————

The cold air stung Hugh's nose as he sucked in a long, deep breath. Rubbing his eyes, he sat up and stretched. The tent was dark and quiet.

Groaning, he reached over to pat the empty bundle of blankets across the tent.

"Damn," he muttered.

Hugh kicked his way free of the cocoon he had made in his sleep. He was in a foul mood as he shoved his frozen toes into his boots. He emerged from the tent to find the morning clear and crisp. It almost cheered him.

He turned immediately to his left and looked up into the dense limbs of the great tree they had made camp by. Hearing rustling, he stepped closer.

"What've I been telling you?" he growled, ducking between huge leaves.

He could hear boots scraping against bark.

"*Rhys,* come down. We'll be late again."

"Who cares?" echoed down the tree.

"I do. C'mon, we have a job to do."

Rhys's upside down head suddenly dropped in front of him. Hugh rolled his eyes.

"It's boring."

"It's important."

Giving his best moan, Rhys crossed his arms. His face was turning a bright red from the blood rushing to his head.

Hugh was considering grabbing him when finally Rhys hauled himself up, unhooked his legs, and jumped down. He gave Hugh a dirty look as he marched out from under the tree.

"You can't just do what you want all the time. Not anymore," Hugh said, shoving his hands into his pockets.

Rhys gave him a sidelong glare. "The other kids don't have to work."

"They're going to go to school, once we get it built. You wanna go to school instead?"

Rhys's nose wrinkled.

"This is stupid," he insisted after a few minutes of silent walking.

"What?"

"We should be allowed to go where we want. This is supposed to be our new home but they just have us trapped here. Shouldn't we explore?"

Hugh could see Rhys's impatience and frustration written in his hard frown.

"We will," he said, "soon. We have to get everything set up first."

Rhys just glared off into the distance, and Hugh knew he didn't like that answer. Rhys liked action, never planned very much for the future. He didn't understand doing things for the long-run and hated the word "later." He heard him mutter under his breath, but only caught "stupid" now and again.

Deciding not to push him anymore, Hugh contented himself with a silent walk to work. It had been a while, but he remembered well that it was best not to push Rhys too hard. If he did, he would probably get snapped at.

The deconstruction team was making good progress with the first stages of repurposing. The *Mayflower* would be the first ship to devote her outer hull to the construction of buildings, some of which were already underway. These had gone to General Hammond as her headquarters and other military buildings. Soon they would begin taking apart more of the walls and inner rooms and converting them into small homes and apartments.

Hugh was working with Saranov, his former mentor, on something he thought much more interesting. It was time for the engines to find their new home as generators. Since the *Mayflower*'s engines were the only ones that hadn't shown signs of malfunctioning, General Hammond was anxious to implement them first in the powering of the new colony.

It was a surreal experience walking into the former starship. She was beginning to seem skeletal, especially from the outside. All up and down the starboard side crews worked to cut off measured metal strips.

They walked past the deconstruction crews and headed into the more familiar innards of the ship, entering the elevator Hugh had taken every day for seven years. It took them up to the engine room.

It was much quieter than it had been during

the journey. No ear plugs required. The engines were all running below ten percent of maximum output, having very little to power for the time being.

Hugh caught sight of the scraggily head of Mikhail Saranov and headed for him. Saranov smiled in greeting.

"Almost on time this morning," he said.

"Just adjusting," Hugh replied.

Saranov looked from Hugh to Rhys and back. His piercing blue eyes narrowed slightly. Hugh never could hide much from Saranov, but he didn't want to say anything. Rhys was in a bad enough mood as it was.

"Shall we?" the weathered engineer said, rolling up his sleeves.

Hugh nodded, happy to get to work.

In truth, the new world was overwhelming. Being outdoors again was great, but it was new. Seven years of metal everything and before that eleven of dead, dry Earth made this new, green, lush planet very alien to Hugh. Getting back to work doing what he knew, what he had been trained for, was comforting.

It was also nice to know that while the world outside would present new challenges every day, his work would remain the same. The engine and surrounding rooms were to be the only original structures left standing; converting them only slightly, it would stand in the center of the new colony as a power plant, as would the engine rooms of the other three starships.

Work promised to be an exciting challenge that day. They were going to start converting the first of the six auxiliary engines. Cracking his knuckles, Hugh followed Saranov to work.

It was a delicate process. They had to know which wires to reroute and which subfuses to cut off. An hour trickled by, then two before they could even begin thinking about attaching the first output cable.

Rhys shadowed Saranov the whole while, the

engineer explaining to him the intricacies of the engines. He was in the learning stages, just as Hugh had been, and Hugh hoped Saranov's teachings would help center Rhys. True, engineering certainly wasn't one of Rhys's strengths, but it was something for him to do. If left to his own devices, Rhys would rather get up to—

"Damn it all!" Saranov said. "Where'd he go?"

Hugh pushed the safety goggles up onto his forehead and stood.

"What d'you . . . ?"

Rhys was gone.

Saranov looked over at Hugh with a disappointed look. He crossed his arms over his chest.

Yanking the goggles off, Hugh said, "I'll get him."

"You're not going to get through to him this way."

Hugh waved off Saranov as he jogged towards the elevator. He tapped his foot impatiently during the ride down.

The sun was bright, and he squinted, his hand out over his head as he walked briskly from the starship. His eyes were everywhere, looking for Rhys. He tried to stifle his panic.

He nodded awkwardly as he passed an officer. Knowing it would do more harm than good to let the military know about Rhys wandering off, Hugh walked as quickly as he could away from the military quadrant and headed for the residential one. Rhys liked it there.

When he came upon the tent city, he headed up to the first person he came across, a woman with long bronze hair. Trying not to pick at his thumb, he asked if she had seen a boy with dark hair and freckles pass through.

"Yes, about ten minutes ago. He headed that way, I think."

"Thanks!"

Hugh left her before groaning. Rhys was headed for the perimeter.

He went quickly, thankful that everyone seemed too busy to notice him in his military-issued clothes.

Chewing the inside of his bottom lip, Hugh came to the perimeter.

The perimeter at first sight didn't seem like much. Every twenty yards or so was a disc-shaped device standing fifteen feet on a thin, stake-like piece of metal. Between each device was an almost translucent blue field.

Hugh knew better than to try and waltz through it. At the least it would trigger an alarm and he would have a whole squad on top of him. At worst it would fry him in less than two seconds.

He looked about, trying to figure out if Rhys had gotten that far, and if so, if he had gotten any farther. He tried not to groan again when he saw a tall pair of trees not far away, one inside the perimeter, the other out. Some of the branches looked treaded.

He couldn't decide which to do—pick at his thumb, chew his lip, bite a nail—as he paced. Half of him wanted to let Rhys fend for himself, come back when he got cold and hungry. But then he wondered if Rhys would make it back. His stomach sank. He couldn't leave him out there.

Grumbling about Rhys never listening, Hugh stalked over to the tree. It took several minutes and several attempts before he was climbing. Telling himself not to look down, he hauled himself up and up and up until finally he was above the line of the perimeter.

He sucked in a breath, feeling as if he had left his stomach back on the ground.

His mind was ablaze, this feeling all too reminiscent of Rhys going somewhere headlong, with no regrets, and Hugh following behind, cautious. At almost nineteen, Hugh didn't enjoy feeling like a duckling again.

He lay on the long limb for a good while, telling himself he needed to do it. But he couldn't move. He stared at the ground, looking increasingly far away, and felt frozen in place.

"Okay, okay, here we go. Three"—he sucked

in a breath—"two"—he shimmied as far out as he could and planted his feet—"one."

He went sailing into the opposite tree, smacking into coarse bark. He clawed into it, finding a hold. Clinging there as he tried to make his heart stop racing, Hugh thought about the many ways he was going to kill Rhys. The climb down was made quicker by the slick leaves of the tree, and he hit the ground with an unpleasant *smack*.

Slow to his feet, Hugh rubbed his hip, grimacing. "Rhys?"

It was eerily silent. Hugh pressed on as quietly as he could, jumping at the slightest sound. They knew nothing about what was beyond the perimeter.

He swallowed hard. Swearing he heard a rustle, Hugh looked about.

"Rhys, c'mon. This wasn't even funny on Earth."

Suddenly feeling like the lost kid in a dark alleyway, Hugh stumbled, his hands shaking. He almost couldn't remember the way back to the perimeter.

There was a rumbling sound to his left, and he froze. From the underbrush stalked a dark body, clad in glistening purple scales. He could make little out other than large slit green eyes watching him.

For a fleeting moment he wondered if it was a native, but the growl of the beast told him it was something much worse.

The creature burst from the bushes, its blue mouth wide and snarling. It landed before him, scaly muscle bright in the afternoon sun. Spikes ran down its spine, leading to a four-pronged tail. Huge haunches seemed ready to launch the creature while long claws pawed the earth.

He stumbled backwards, his hands up. They were shaking.

Those green eyes looked him up and down as the beast stalked forwards, its jowls pulled tight across jaws with two rows of teeth apiece. Its head lowered, haunches winding up for a pounce.

With a great roar it leapt in the air towards him. He cried out, but he couldn't do anything.

A hand gripped the back of his collar and threw him to the ground. *Bang, bang, bang!* echoed through the trees.

He was trembling when he dared open an eye. He lay flat on his back, looking up at the blue sky. Someone stood next to him, slinging an automatic into a holster on her back.

"Elena!"

She looked down at him. "Honestly, what would you do without me?"

----

"You're lucky I was on patrol," Elena said as she and Hugh walked quickly away from the gleaming purple carcass.

His face was downturned in apology. He shoved his hands into his jacket pockets as they headed back to the perimeter.

She didn't mean to be gruff with him, but honestly, she had lost count of how many times he had made trouble for her. Though, she had to admit, it was pretty amusing watching him jump between trees.

Jerking a thumb over her shoulder, she said, "*That's* why I wanted you to take this." She shoved a hand gun against his chest.

He paled, his hands slow to take it up. He shook his head.

"No, I . . . "

He handed it back to her.

She scowled, insisting, "You have to protect yourself."

He shook his head again.

Elena stopped, surprising him. She got in his face and demanded, "What if I'm not there next time, huh? You would've made a very nice meal for that *thing*."

Hugh's mouth was open but nothing came out.

She snorted and stalked towards the perimeter.

Inching as close as she could to it, she held up her arm with the gauntlet strapped on it. A keypad flashed onto the face and she input that day's combination.

The section of perimeter flashed white-blue and then disappeared. Waving a hand at Hugh, she hurried them through, the perimeter going back up behind them.

"I'm sorry," he said as they headed back towards camp. "I didn't mean to put you out."

She sighed. She was perfectly content to be aggravated with him, but he made it hard.

"What were you doing out there?" She peered at him. "Let me guess. He's missing?"

Hugh winced. "I would've told you, but . . . "

She put her hands on her hips. "Where was he last seen? I could have a squad put together to—"

"No, no, don't. I don't want them to go back on everything. They've been bending a lot of rules for me and Rhys."

"You know I'm going to have to report this. They'll want to know why I lowered the perimeter."

He looked at her pleadingly. "Cover for me?"

She tried to stop herself from looking at him, knew she would give in if she did. She tried focusing on his nose, but his eyes, pleading and uncomfortably blue, were right there.

"*Fine.*"

Hugh smiled. "Thank you."

When they made it back into the residential quadrant, Hugh began looking about.

"D'you think you'd have access to a scanner of some sort? I know the direction he went, but—"

"No need," Elena said with an internal groan.

"What? Why?"

She pointed. "He's right there."

In a wide grass-like patch were a brood of kids kicking around a tattered soccer ball. Rhys was at their center, deftly defending the ball from several attacking feet.

Elena put her hands on her hips again and

decided to be angry for Hugh. He stood unmoving beside her, clenching then unclenching his fists.

"I'm gonna knock his head in," she grumbled. "You get one side and I'll take the other."

She gave him a sidelong grin. That was more like it.

Still they didn't move towards Rhys, and it finally dawned on Elena that Hugh was more relieved than angry. She couldn't fathom why, but it must've been a sibling thing. She didn't have any, not on Terra Nova, not on Earth, and she was beginning to think that was a good thing after seeing what Rhys put Hugh through, both his absence during the journey and now his rebellion in the colony.

"I could have him put in the brig for a night," she suggested.

Hugh grinned at that. "He'd get out. Somehow."

"So what're you gonna do?"

He shrugged his heavy shoulders. "Talk to him."

"Yeah, because that's working real well."

"Well do you have any suggestions?"

"Yeah. The brig."

Hugh finally laughed, and she felt a bit better. He seemed so tired lately with the added worry. Hugh had always been a quiet, solemn person, but having to care for someone who was so capricious wore him down.

Yet it wasn't her place, she thought, to point this out.

Suddenly there was a small buzzing sound and a wide projection appeared above the city center. The same projection popped up several places, all some distance away.

General Hammond looked out at them.

"Good afternoon everyone," she said.

From the look of it she was standing in her headquarters. Elena could see Colonel Klein's meaty shoulder in the shot.

"I hope you all have settled this past month as we make New Haven our new home. I would like to update you now on our plans for the foreseeable future:

"Deconstruction is on schedule and within another month we hope to be relocating individuals into the first apartment complexes. Small houses will be completed soon afterwards and anyone wishing to claim one should notify us as soon as possible. Upon completion of housing we will begin on the market quadrant where all non-residential and non-military or industrial buildings will be located. Job applications will become available soon.

"Secondly, we are pleased to announce the opening of our first school. All children of elementary age and not already assigned to an apprenticeship should report there tomorrow morning at oh-eight-hundred hours."

Elena swore she heard a collective groan from the surrounding kids.

"Next, to deal with the loss of one fifth of our supplies, we will be sending out scouting and foraging parties. Our able military is well equipped to handle the surrounding terrain, but any fit volunteers are welcome to submit their names. Rest assured, these parties are solely for the further understanding of our new home. They will seek out answers on how we may sustain ourselves for generations from the planet rather than the ships.

"Which brings me to the last point. To learn more about Terra Nova, Dr. Oswald and his team will be starting construction on several satellites that will be launched into the planet's lower atmosphere. These will help us take scans and better understand our new home.

"With that I'll let you get back to your business. If you have any questions, please direct them towards the appropriate officer. Good day."

And with another buzzing sound the projection disappeared.

Everyone took a long moment to recover, the flood of information washing over them.

Nearby Elena heard a group of women talking.

"Well that was a nice way to put everything we already knew," said one.

"She didn't mention anything about an election," said another.

"She never does."

And she never will, Elena thought.

She shifted her weight, drawing Hugh's gaze. They looked at each other for a long moment but said nothing, knowing full well where talking would get them.

General Hammond had gotten quite used to issuing orders for the past seven years. What was unsettling wasn't that she wanted to continue giving orders, but that they all, Elena, Hugh, all of those who had been awake, were too used to following them.

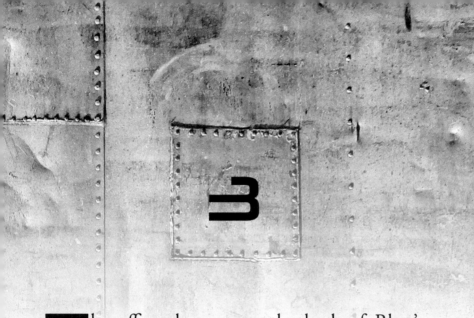

3

The officer hung onto the back of Rhys's collar to make sure he didn't go anywhere, so Rhys had to content himself with crossing his arms and pouting.

Hugh answered the door, his eyes wide in surprise. He looked from Rhys, to the officer, then swallowed hard.

"He was found trying to jump the perimeter. Again," said the officer, roughly shoving Rhys into the apartment.

Hugh's face fell while Rhys's soured. The military certainly wasn't endearing itself to Rhys. Yeah, they had caught him. This time. He had been out past the perimeter at least a dozen times and he had been fine. He couldn't understand why they were so upset about it.

Hugh's hand dug into his shoulder as he held him in place, knowing Rhys was liable to bolt.

"I'm so sorry. It won't—"

"This isn't how the general wants things," said the officer, leaning towards Hugh. "We're supposed to be getting off to a good start. This isn't a good start."

Hugh nodded, paler than usual.

Rhys was sneering up at the officer when he looked down at him. Rhys's expression didn't change.

"Rules are there for a reason, son," he said. "We can't let the one slide when it endangers the whole."

Feeling like the setup the military had going now didn't sound much different than that aboard the starships, Rhys crossed his arms and remained silent. At least until Hugh prodded between his shoulder blades.

"Yup."

Realizing that was all he was going to get, the officer nodded gruffly and left them.

Hugh tugged Rhys into the apartment and shut the door.

Rhys wriggled out from underneath Hugh's hand. His brother's touch, once so familiar, exactly like his own, was different. It wasn't just that it was bigger. It was the touch of a stranger.

Rhys stalked into the main room and sat down on the bench, the only adornment. Hugh had put their names in for a small house, but hadn't got it. Most were reserved for the couples who had met through the regime's matchmaking services. The thought made Rhys's nose wrinkle. Hugh managed to get them this apartment instead; it was larger than most, a double rather than a single. There was an anteroom into a living room and a small kitchen off to the side.

What was best about it was that they both had their own rooms. Rhys had already made a suitable mess in his own, his old Earth clothes and possessions strewn about properly. They had finally gotten their luggage while moving in and it had been surreal sifting through the items he had packed ages ago. Nothing of Hugh's fit anymore.

Hugh was pacing, pulling a hand through his hair. It was rather unkempt and fell in wayward, curly tendrils. What irked Rhys most was the shadow of a beard darkening Hugh's jaw line.

"This can't keep happening, Rhys," he said finally.

Rhys rolled his eyes. Not this again.

"It's not a big deal."

"It is! If you keep getting in trouble, they'll punish you."

"Well they can't put me in jail. It's not built yet," Rhys laughed.

Hugh's dark look silenced him. He sniffed.

"Why d'you do it? What's so damn interesting that you can't just do what you're told?"

"Everything's more interesting! Everyone would go out there if they knew how awesome everything is. Hugh, there're trees bigger than buildings! And up to the north—*snow*. Do you know how cold it is? It bites and it's just so, so . . . well great. It's real. I know you'd like it too if you'd just—"

Hugh was shaking his head. "You're not supposed to."

Rhys was stung by Hugh's determined denial. Usually Rhys could talk him into anything—yeah it took a bit of persuasion, yeah he almost always said no first, but in the end he would join Rhys on whatever adventure he had in mind.

The person frowning down at him wasn't his fellow adventurer. It was an adult. The realization hit him like a kick in the gut, nearly winding him.

"Who says?" he croaked.

"The military."

"Well who put them in charge?" Rhys spat.

Hugh's mouth opened but nothing came out. Rhys nodded triumphantly.

"It's just how things are," Hugh said. "You'd better learn that."

"I can't believe you! You're like some brain-washed drone, believing everything they tell you!"

"They got us through the years. They'll get us through this too."

"Oh c'mon, it's not like it was that—"

"You don't know what it was like!"

Hugh's eyes were aflame like Rhys had never seen. What was scarier was the immeasurable pain hidden beneath that fire, the pain of a brutal, bleak life. He watched, disturbed, at the swiftness and ferocity with which Hugh smothered the flame, pushed the emotion down until it was buried deep.

He pouted from being shouted at.

"*I* know this is wrong," he said. He jumped to his feet. "They're not the boss of me." He muscled his way past Hugh. "And neither are you."

"Rhys, don't—"

*Slam.*

The crisp mountain air filled Rhys's lungs as he dashed down the stairs and out onto the narrow lane leading from the apartment complex. He knew he was safe for now—Hugh hated confrontation and wouldn't follow him when it only meant a fight. At least, he hoped not.

"What does he know anyway?" he muttered to himself, slowing as he made it into the center of the residential quadrant.

He liked it there, among his people. Civilians—the sleepers—milled about doing their daily business, dressed in their old Earth clothes rather than the stark military uniform. Rhys thought Hugh's liable to swallow him whole.

For a while he just wandered. He liked getting to stretch his legs and be under the wide blue sky. The colony was growing day by day. The *Mayflower* was completely deconstructed; the only piece that remained was the power plant he and Hugh worked at, which had once been the engine rooms. The ship had served as enough to make half of the residential buildings and several other necessary structures. Another ship would be devoted to finishing the residential district while the other two would go towards factories, warehouses, stores, two upper level schools, and even a library. While there would be no books, the central intelligence unit would be there with the entirety of Earth-knowledge stored inside. Or at least that's what Hugh had told him.

Soon he tired of the increasingly familiar dirt streets and changed course. He had been sloppy that morning. Hadn't been watching his back.

He slipped into an alleyway, making sure the shadows covered him completely before prowling around the corner and heading to the perimeter. It was a bit of a hike without much cover, most of the natural foliage having been cleared for the colony's development. He had hated watching them fell the great trees. All that way to see green again, just to destroy it.

He couldn't understand why more people didn't want to go exploring. They had come all this way just to coop themselves up? Though, he had to admit, the military's propaganda about the outside was pretty persuasive—to sum up, anything and everything could kill humans out there. It was an effective enough message to keep most everyone inside the colony. The only people who ventured out were those on assignment. And Rhys.

He headed to one of his less favorite escape points. A steep rock outcropping, the perimeter went over it. Rhys went under. He didn't like having to wriggle, and more than once he had found himself stuck for several hours before he had manage to squirm out. He would much prefer scaling a tree, but those were becoming a rare option.

This time proved easier than others, though he realized that when he finally grew the route would become impossible.

Scrambling out the other side, Rhys dusted himself off and felt weightless. He trotted off into the forest, heading south. He found one of his paths and started down the rocky incline, drawn towards the flatland below.

The vegetation was markedly different here. There were no large trees, though the small clusters of bush-like plants did actually seem like smaller trees. Some of them had spiny bark, and he made sure to give these a wide berth.

He loved everything about this new world. It was everything Earth wasn't. He walked into the clearing in almost perfect silence. Save for the small crunch of his boots over dirt, the world was quiet, still, pristine. He felt very small and liked it.

He stopped near a small mound of rocks. The ground beneath him trembled, rumbled, shook.

Looking south, Rhys beheld a thundering pack of native beasts. They looked like giant turtles, with shells and beaks, but their heads had spikes and their long tails had four prongs. They lumbered on feet with three toes, their small eyes straight ahead as they loped.

What froze him in place were the creatures on top of the beasts. Tall, lithe, painted with red, natives came riding closer.

———————

*"Natives sighted. Natives sighted. Squadron A and C report."*

Elena was on the heels of Sgt. White as they jumped up into the back of a cruiser. The automated voice repeated its message as the squadrons amassed, shouldering weapons and finding transports.

Sgt. White pounded the roof of the cruiser. "All in—let's go!"

The vehicle rumbled around them, purring to life, then leapt forward, screeching out of the hangar. They hung onto straps bolted to the roof as the cruiser careened out of the equipment sector then through the military quadrant.

A large projection appeared in the empty center

space of the vehicle, showing several angles of the southern flatlands and a few readings. The shots were too far away to discern much, but this she could tell: there was a group of natives riding some sort of creatures, and they were headed towards the colony.

"Now listen here and listen good," said the sergeant in her best bark, "we're to hold our ground and defend the colony. I want a nice clean line made, two deep, and we hold. You won't march, you won't shoot until I say otherwise." She gazed across the cruiser at Oscar when she said, "I'm not interested in a bloodbath. Is that understood?"

"Yes, ma'am!"

"Headed through the perimeter," said the driver.

Here the ride got even bumpier, the cruiser speeding over unleveled ground. The soldier to Elena's left slammed into her as they took a sharp turn to avoid a tree.

Once they hit the clearing things smoothed as they sped on.

Elena bit the inside of her bottom lip. She had been trained for this day—she had known since hearing they weren't going to be alone that she would be expected to fire at living targets. She hadn't anticipated the way her stomach rolled at the idea.

She tried to think about anything else, focusing on the small hum of the cruiser. The ride felt like it was dragging on, though it was only mere seconds that trickled by. Looking up, she accidentally caught Oscar's gaze.

He was watching her, saw how uncomfortable she looked, how downturned her mouth was. A small grin played at his lips to see the fear in her.

She straightened, indignant.

Elena and Oscar were both former apprentices of the sergeant, Oscar by assignment and Elena by choice. He had never forgotten or forgiven the favoritism. Not that Elena gave him much reason to like her. She had sensed from the very beginning that they would be enemies. Oscar was a bully, and the worst kind. Sadistic and malicious, he always reveled in her failures. While she certainly didn't find any pleasure from his success, she had never sought to torment him.

The instant the cruiser came to a stop, Sgt. White was shouting in their ears, "Go, go, go!"

Hitting the ground running, Elena followed the soldier in front of her out onto the craggy flatland. They fell in a line beside the cruiser, two deep, and marched forward.

"Ames, right flank!"

Dashing to the outer edge of the line, Elena resumed her defensive position and began moving forward slowly with the rest of the line to her left.

Oscar always belittled Elena's getting the flank assignment, saying it was out of the action. But she didn't mind. From the time she was twelve years old, the sergeant had drilled into her that the flank was the most important assignment—lose the flank and it's as good as over.

They stalked forwards a few yards before Sgt.

White gave the command to halt and hold. They settled in.

It wasn't a long wait. The natives weren't coming fast, their mounts lumbering more than running. The beasts were turtle-like and the natives were long, lean, with swirls of colored skin that shimmered red and mixed with war paint smeared across their faces. They had long, ovular faces with a hairless brow, wide, square eyes, nostrils but no nose, and a lipless mouth. From the looks of them they had only three fingers, two long and a shorter thumb-like one, and their feet, the bulkiest part of them, tapered out from a thin calf to a wide foot with three toes.

Their russet breastplates gleamed in the afternoon sun, and other assorted archaic weapons were strewn across their saddles, backs, and laps. As the two groups came into view of each other, the centermost rider held up a slim hand in a fist. The natives halted.

They were more than two hundred yards away,

but still well within range of the guns. Elena didn't know the reach of their arrows.

They stood there staring at one another, these two species. The human soldiers stayed as still as possible, all remembering the sergeant's orders. Elena knew she couldn't be the only one breathless at the sight of the natives—something humans had only once dreamed about now stood opposite them, real as day.

It was because of the eerie silence that Elena almost jumped out of her skin at a small rustling beside her. Throwing her gaze behind the mound of rocks she stood beside, she looked wildly about, wondering if she had lost the flank.

An eye peered at her. She leaned back slowly. Two eyes. A heaving chest. Brown hair.

"You've gotta be kidding me," she hissed.

Rhys looked at her pleadingly. "Don't tell Hugh."

Glaring, she demanded, "What the hell d'you think you're doing out here?"

He shrugged. "Thought I'd take a walk."

She took a ragged breath, trying to swallow the need to shoot him. It didn't work. "Do you have any idea—"

*Bang, bang!*

Sgt. White held her gun skyward, let the shots' echoes pulse out into the silence.

The natives flinched but didn't retreat.

Readjusting her gun against her shoulder, Elena tried to focus instead of letting her brain conjure up elaborate punishments for Rhys.

"Do you promise?" he whispered.

"No."

"C'mon, please? I'll owe you one."

She threw him a venomous look over her shoulder. "Don't you think? D'you have any idea how devastated Hugh would be if you got hurt?"

"He worries too much."

"He doesn't worry enough! Where the hell do you think you are? This isn't playtime."

"I didn't know they would be out here. And besides, they're awesome!"

"You just don't get it, do you?"

He seemed bemused by that, but Elena didn't have time to explain as the native leader began shifting in its saddle. The warrior looked about at its troops, surveyed the humans, and gave an order. Its voice, while faint, was an interesting sound, the syllables it spoke sharp and undulating. The beasts moved forward.

"Ramirez, Cox, with me!"

Sgt. White's first and then two more guns went off, shots littering the ground several yards in front of the native line. Dirt flew in the air, the sound ricocheting off into the cold air. The beasts stopped, threw their heads.

The warriors cried out, went for their weapons, notched arrows.

Sgt. White gave the order. Elena shouldered her gun, trained her sights on the narrow chest of a warrior four from the center. She took a ragged breath.

There was shouting. She listened. Not theirs. The leader was giving more orders, its voice sharp, stern, its fist in the air again. It seemed to be trying to get control again.

For a moment it looked like this was going to happen. There was going to be a firefight. She closed an eye, focusing on the fourth from the center.

More shouting. Whatever the leader said had some effect. Finally the bowstrings slackened. The leader put both hands up, palms bear-faced, rotated them once, twice.

The beasts began to back up, heading the way they had come but backwards.

None of the soldiers relaxed until the natives were out of sight. Then they breathed.

Lowering her gun, Elena rubbed a temple. That had been too close, and she didn't like how shaken up she felt.

In her relief, she had an overwhelming desire to get Rhys in trouble. However, taking him to Hugh wouldn't exactly accomplish that. All Hugh would do was blame himself more, try harder, and in doing so push Rhys further away. Not to mention, she wasn't sure if it was necessarily any of her business, minus Rhys breaking the law.

Rhys was looking at her with big eyes, his breaths coming in short gasps. She didn't even want to think what she would have had to do if that had ended up a firefight.

"You've been nothing but a pain in the ass," Elena hissed, running a hand through her hair, "and you don't deserve it. But I won't tell Hugh. For now."

Rhys grinned, relieved.

"Thanks! I definitely—"

"Once we've started heading back, get up to the colony. And you stay put. If I ever catch you out here again I'll use you for target practice."

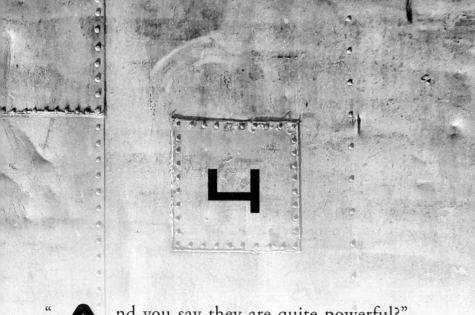

"**A**nd you say they are quite powerful?"

"Yes, Golden One. They have weapons, powerful weapons, that are unlike our own."

"You saw them use these weapons?" questioned Elder Vasya, walking to the front.

The messenger, one of Ondra's warriors, shifted.

"Yes, Wise One. As I said, they met us in the field, but nothing happened."

Elder Vasya nodded. "If nothing happened, then how can we say for certain they are powerful?"

"Do you want a death toll, Elder? Will that satisfy you?"

The Red Hall fell silent, surprised at the dark words from the *mara*.

Zeneba's heavy head leaned on her hand. It certainly wasn't good news that the messenger had brought back, only confirmation of her many fears. For the moment she was letting herself wallow in her gloom.

Elder Vasya crossed his arms over his narrow chest. "Forgive me, Golden One, but this news can only mean one thing—the demons are gaining a foothold in the north."

"I heard him just as well as you, Wise One," Zeneba said.

She had to stop herself from slumping down in her seat. It was moments like this that she wished Elder Zhora wasn't a Skywatcher. His attendance at council meetings was infrequent, having to commune with Nahara and Undin, their beloved sun gods. He spent most of his time in the Cloud Gardens, trying to divine some wisdom from the Sunned Ones.

Elder Zhora's seat was instead filled by Zaynab, who looked utterly bored. His eyelids were drooping, and more than once she had to swat at him when the Elders weren't looking to keep him awake.

Sighing, Zeneba lifted her head. "We will stay the course." She addressed to the messenger, "Ride back to Chieftain Ura as soon as you can with my promise of anything he needs. And tell your leader to continue learning what he can about these demons."

The warrior bowed to her and headed from the Hall.

Elder Vasya stayed put, his mouth a thin line. "It seems they are yet to be established," he said. "Now is the time to strike, lest they build stronger fortifications. To let them be is to invite them to stay."

"Thank you, Elder. I shall bear that in mind."

Elder Vasya's eyes narrowed before he stormed out of the Hall, sore from such a dismissal.

Zaynab snickered. Zeneba gave him a scathing look from the corner of her eye.

Most of her council exited the Red Hall. There was much to see to; some were occupied with securing food lines, others with overseeing the strengthening of fortifications, while others felt sure to find a solution through prayer.

She was so tired. Her eyes stung with every blink. Yet whenever she closed her eyes, what she saw was much worse: bloodshed, pain, loss. She heard screams in her ears and determined not to sleep at all lest the sound drive her mad.

Yaro cleared his throat.

Sighing, Zeneba turned to face him. She had anticipated this, but that didn't mean she was looking forward to it.

"I wonder, Golden One, if this outfit is as effective as you wanted," he said, careful of his phrasing.

"It's doing what I want, yes," she replied.

"Leading a party out into the open field as he did—"

"Ondra didn't engage them, like I ordered. He sends me back intelligence, like I ordered. You question him, but I'm starting to think you're truly questioning me."

She knew Yaro didn't deserve her foul mood, but he certainly wasn't alleviating it. It frustrated her to be told constantly that she was mismanaging things. If not from Yaro, then from Elder Vasya, and if not from him, then from others on the council. She could see the trepidation in her people's eyes—they were anxious and sought firm leadership. Yet Zeneba could not stomach the idea of sending Charneki off to war.

Slumping down in her seat, she removed the heavy ornaments of the *lahn-nahar*, the official symbols of her queenship, and put the jade gauntlets and gold circlet in her lap.

Zaynab prodded her. Turning to him with a glare didn't dampen his grin.

"Perhaps I could go help Ondra," he said. "I'm

getting good you know—or you would know if you ever came to practice anymore . . . "

There was so much in his statement that she didn't know where to start.

"I've much to see to," she said, growing angry when she saw him mouthing her words as she said them.

He only looked mildly sheepish. "That's what you keep saying."

She waved her hand before her. "And this doesn't seem like something I should see to?"

"You can't always be thinking about these things."

"Of course I can—whether I want to or not. It's a *mara*'s duty."

"Well then take a break from being *mara*. You worry too much."

"I can't 'take a break!' I'm *mara* now until the day I die—or don't you remember the coronation ceremony?"

"I remember," he said, beginning to sulk.

They sat in silence, both unwilling to leave, with an enormously uncomfortable Yaro, trying to stay out of it, standing by.

Zaynab clapped his ankles together.

Zeneba fiddled with the gold chain of her circlet.

"Will you at least consider it?" he asked finally.

"Consider what?"

"Letting me go join Ondra's outfit. I could be useful."

"And how could you be useful, Zaynab? You're just a *mahar*."

Yaro winced, and Zaynab's mouth fell open.

Zaynab's iridescent skin turned a deep, saddened blue, and he jumped from his seat, running from the Red Hall.

Zeneba's own mouth had fallen open, unable to believe what she said. She tried to make her jaw move, form words of apology, but nothing came out, and Zaynab disappeared.

Groaning, her head slumped down into her hands again. From the dark recess she said, "Yaro, will you see to him please? Make sure he doesn't try to walk all the way to the tundra."

"Yes, Golden One."

As she listened to the retreating echoes of Yaro's feet, she realized with no small amount of dark humor that she had hurt most of those she cared about in one fell swoop. The *lahn-nahar* in her lap felt incredibly heavy.

---

Hugh wiped the sticky sweat off his brow with the already grimy rag. The time blinked on his gauntlet, telling him it was quitting time, and he dreamt of little else than a shower.

Standing, he stretched out his stiff back. Saranov gave him a sympathetic grin.

"Didn't think we'd be getting two projects at a time," he said.

That was the truth. With the general's announcement of the satellites, Saranov and a team had been put together to start construction. General Hammond would have had them wholly devoted to the satellite were she not reminded by Saranov that the generators still needed finishing. Without them there wouldn't be the energy to power homes, plants, or the satellite's construction.

Hugh shook his head. "Better busy than bored."

Saranov clapped his back and chuckled. "Off you go. You've done your time."

Hugh didn't argue, though he always did feel rather guilty leaving Saranov to continue on alone. It wasn't that Saranov had to—he just did. During the journey, Hugh would have stayed with him, would have been happy to put in the extra hours, but both of them knew things weren't like they were on the ship.

Shoving his hands in his pockets as he made his way towards the elevator, Hugh silently pleaded that the trust he had shown Rhys hadn't been abused. He had given his brother the day off, told him to have fun but not get into trouble.

Rhys had been somewhat reasonable lately. He had only broken curfew a handful of times, and he hadn't shown up on their doorstep escorted by an officer again. Hugh didn't know what had gotten into him. He was suspicious.

"Straight home," the soldier told him, as he did every night, when Hugh exited the plant.

Hugh paused only long enough to nod. The curfew the military had enacted after the native sighting was strict. The city square, in the center of the residential quadrant, had been forcibly cleared the first few nights. Now all lights were off without fuss at dark.

While he didn't think the natives as much of a problem as the military made them out to be, Hugh certainly didn't share Rhys's obvious fascination. He was always asking questions, trying to determine if Hugh had been told something he hadn't. The official statement was that the natives were, for now, sticking to their village just beyond the horizon. No immediate action was to be taken except for upping defenses. Hugh truly didn't know any more than that.

Personally Hugh wanted everything to be quiet. He wanted a quiet life, a real life. He wanted to get to know the person he had become on that starship voyage, for he hadn't had the time to think about it aboard. He wanted to get to know the person his brother was becoming, for every day it felt like Rhys was growing away from him.

Realizing what he was thinking, Hugh did what he always chose to do and buried his worries. Pushed and pushed until it was numb. He was left only with a slight choked feeling.

He hopped up the steps and strode to their apartment's front door. He sucked in a breath, put his hand on the scanner. It flashed green and the locks *clicked*.

He was welcomed by a dark apartment, and when he stepped in and the lights turned on, he found it empty as well.

"Rhys?" He didn't know why he whispered.

The main room stood silent.

He walked over to the door of Rhys's room and knocked, repeating his name. Nothing.

Hugh took a step back and picked at his thumb, trying not to conjure up all the various ways Rhys could be in mortal peril.

A small noise sent him whirling around, and he and Rhys met each other's startled gaze.

Rhys was in the process of climbing through the back window and immediately looked guilty.

"You've got to be kidding me!" Hugh cried as Rhys stumbled into the apartment.

"It's not what it looks like," Rhys protested, closing the window.

"So you weren't just jumping the perimeter? Why should I believe you? What if you'd been caught?"

"I *wasn't*! I was just in town!"

"Right," Hugh scoffed. "That's why you decided to come in the back way."

Rhys looked anywhere but at him. "I thought you'd be asleep."

"Because the front door makes *so* much noise."

Rhys glowered. "I don't have to stand here and take this. Not from *you.*"

He made to stomp into his room, but Hugh blocked his way. Both were surprised.

"You've gotta stop this, Rhys. Stop acting like a kid."

He looked at Hugh venomously. "*I am* a kid. You're the one who's not."

Hugh's jaw clenched, and he tried changing tactics. "You've got duties, responsibilities here, and you have to abide by the law."

"I didn't go anywhere!"

"I don't believe you."

"Well that's your problem, not mine."

Hugh didn't quite know why he was stoking the flame, for that was exactly what he was doing. He knew Rhys. He knew how he would react. But something inside him, something desperate, wanted to establish some sort of authority. He was older now, but it was more than that—he wanted to finally be Rhys's equal.

"Rhys, just . . . " Hugh rubbed his weary eyes. "Just try and understand for a minute. I'm trying to do the best I can here—I'm trying to take care of the both of us, and I can't—"

"Nobody asked you!" Rhys roared. "I don't need you to take care of me!"

Hugh paced a moment, unsure what to do with his hands. Both his thumbs were already bleeding, the grime on his hands stinging the small wounds. Finally finding suitable words, he turned back to his brother.

"Look, you took care of us on Earth. You were strong for the both of us. Now we're here and I understand things a bit better. It's my turn to be strong for us."

"I know plenty. I don't need to be taken care of."

"Rhys, we're brothers, we have to—"

"We're *twins*! We're twins and I'm older. You know I'm thirty minutes older than you!" Hot tears ran down his reddening face. "I'm older, I'm . . . "

"Rhys . . . " Hugh reached out a hand to have it slapped away.

"Whatever."

Rhys marched into his room and slammed the door behind him.

Hugh let him go, too stunned to stop him. He hadn't realized . . .

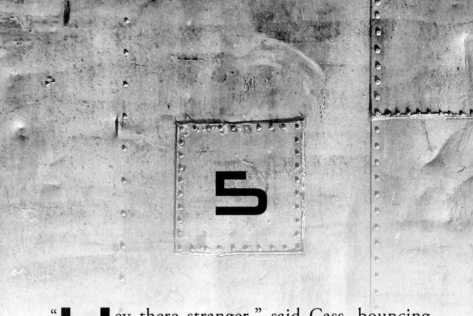

**5**

"Hey there stranger," said Cass, bouncing up to him.

Hugh smiled. "Hey yourself."

He had seen a lot less of his friends than he would have liked, Cassandra Tran especially—he had of course seen Elena in some unfortunate run-ins. Aboard ship they had become inseparable except for the last year when Hugh and Saranov were transferred to one and then a second malfunctioning ship. He had hoped to catch up for lost time when they landed, but that hadn't been the case so far.

"Fancy seeing you here," she said, throwing her

arms up to gesture at the high walls of the former engine room.

"How've you been?"

"Oh, you know. Overworked. How 'bout you?" She peered at him. "I hear things aren't going as . . . smoothly as you wanted."

Hugh hoped his face didn't change. He tried his best to smile. "We're getting on."

He could never lie to Cass, so he didn't know why he was trying. It was out of character that she didn't prod him until he fessed up.

"Have you seen Elena lately?" he asked.

She took the hook. "Yup, about a week ago. She certainly seems well suited to her new job. She always was a brute."

They smiled at that as they walked over to their project. The satellite was coming along nicely and, if all went as planned, would be ready in only a few short days. Dr. Oswald, the scientist who had discovered Terra Nova and now head of the science department, had been overseeing the construction himself.

"He's feeling a little under the weather today though," Cass explained to Saranov, "but he said I'd be all right to look over the final touch-ups. Don't worry, he wouldn't miss launch."

"He just might," boomed a voice from the elevator.

The group of scientists and engineers turned to find General Hammond and her entourage entering the engine room.

"Unless he gets down here quick," the general said, striding towards the group.

There was a hush, no one quite sure what to say.

"General, this is a nice . . . " tried one of the engineers. He couldn't quite finish.

"I hear the satellite's operational," she said. "I'm here to see that it successfully launches. Today."

The team looked at her in surprise.

Saranov cleared his throat. "General, we still have a few tests to run before—"

"Then run them. And then have this thing up in the air by midday."

Saranov balked. "That's just not possible."

The general turned a cold, steely eye onto him. "That's an order, Saranov. Our enemy is on the move and we need to know all we possibly can about them."

"The satellite wasn't meant for surveillance!" Cass protested. She turned white as a sheet realizing what she had done and shrank back under the general's withering gaze.

"It was meant for many things," the general said, her voice chillingly even. Her eyes flicked back to Saranov. "You heard me. I want this thing up. Now."

"Surely we should wait for nightfall," Saranov tried. "Something like this could stir up the natives. We don't know what they'll do."

"It's a chance we have to take. We're blind

right now—that's what this satellite's for. It's our eyes. I'm tired of being in the dark. This will send a message to them. After this, they won't come within a click of our perimeter."

"We don't know that."

"Saranov. I gave you an order. Are you and I going to have problems again?"

Both their eyes narrowed, and Hugh's stomach rolled. Saranov had already received some rough punishment for spreading what the general had labeled 'mutinous slander' during their time aboard one of the failing ships.

Saranov straightened. "No, ma'am."

"Right then. To work."

The general whirled around and headed back to the elevator, leaving her armed guard behind her. The soldiers stood like statues, their gazes hard and distrustful.

Saranov clapped Hugh's shoulder, and he found his mentor's face heavier and more lined than it had been a moment ago. Saranov gave him a nod.

The team numbly set to work, the guards watching on.

"This is crazy," Cass muttered to him under her breath.

"What can we do?"

---

Lying still wasn't one of Elena's strong suits. She didn't always have the urge to fidget, but now that she wasn't supposed to, the desire was overwhelming. The piece of hair she liked to twirl now and again around her fingers got more tantalizing by the second.

Though, in all honesty, it wasn't so bad down there. Holed up in a machine gun nest with another soldier, Elena liked the quiet. True, it was a little unnerving, especially when lying next to a gun the size of a person. But the crisp smell of the dirt was soothing.

They had made a nice cut in the earth to create

a small hole for the gun, covered then by grayish-green canvas to imitate rocks and foliage. It was decent cover. There was a whole line of nests now ranged about in a semi-circle, protecting the southern side of New Haven. Extending past the perimeter, it was the first line of defense against the "native threat" as General Hammond called it.

"Aw damn," murmured the soldier, Terrance Knight, next to her.

"Hmn?"

He nodded at his gauntlet.

Elena looked down at her own to watch the video feed playing on it. There was a lump in her throat as she watched a squadron of natives, again riding those turtle-like creatures, unwittingly heading right towards them.

They came at a cautious pace, certainly not charging, making the decision of what to do more difficult.

"Should we fire a warning shot?" she asked.

Terry shook his head. "They're not very close—"

Elena was startled by the sound of pounding feet and turned towards the opening of the nest just in time to see Sgt. White's face poking in.

"What's the—"

"Ready that thing," said the sergeant. "Warning shot on my mark."

Terry jumped on the gun, having to put his weight behind aiming it at the sky.

Elena finally caught Sgt. White's gaze and gave her a quizzical look.

"All hell's about to break loose," said the sergeant. "Fire!"

Elena opened her mouth to ask what that meant but stopped to clap her hands over her ears as Terry dispelled three shots into the empty sky.

The three of them anxiously watched their gauntlets, reading the natives' reactions. Their eyes were wide, looking about for what had caused the thunderous noise, though they seemed less surprised by it a second time.

Elena watched as the leader made a motion

forward and they began moving again, though more warily.

The sergeant groaned. "Dammit."

"What the hell's going on?" Elena demanded.

She got a small glare for her tone, but the sergeant replied, "The satellite's being launched—any minute now."

"*Now?* But they're so close!"

"The general wants to send a message."

Elena knew better than to complain or criticize, especially about the general, so she held in her disdain and waited.

The minutes that trickled by were torturous. The natives drew ever closer, despite Elena mentally willing them to turn back.

Sgt. White was giving the order for another bout of warning shots when a loud rumbling came from New Haven.

"Here we go . . . " the sergeant muttered.

Switching video feeds, Elena watched as the satellite slowly made its way higher and higher, a thick plume of smoke and exhaust trailing behind it. As it gained height and speed, Elena switched back to the natives.

This had startled them, their beasts shifting about and the warriors unsure what to do. The leader barked something and waved its arm about. All of them reached over the backs and withdrew thick bows and long arrows.

"No, no, no! Sergeant, they're gonna—"

A volley of arrows went sailing into the air as Elena's stomach hit the ground. If humans had been firing the arrows, the nest line would have been out of range, but as she watched the arrows arch high and begin their descent, she had the dreadful realization that they were well within the natives' range.

Sgt. White barked into her gauntlet, reporting what was happening while Terry was manning the gun, swinging it about to use its sights. Elena didn't know what to do with herself.

"They're firing at the satellite, repeat they're firing—"

*Plunk.*

An arrow, almost as long as Elena was tall, ripped through the canvas roof of the nest and stuck deep through Terry's back. He was dead instantly.

Elena's hands went ice cold as she stared at Terry.

"I've got a man hit out here—requesting aid and back up! Repeat, I need—"

"Sergeant," came a measured voice, and suddenly General Hammond's head and shoulders were displaying on both of their gauntlets, "you are to hold your ground and defend New Haven. Fire at will. Drive them back."

The general disappeared, and Sgt. White looked up.

"You heard the general," she said tonelessly. "Man the gun—I'll be back in three minutes."

And with that Elena was left alone in a hole in the ground with a dead man. Everything was numb and cold as she put a trembling hand on Terry's shoulder. She had to put her back into pushing him away from the gun, his body not complying easily, for the arrow had him pinned down.

Choking on her gag reflex, Elena hauled herself up against the butt of the gun, her shoulder pressed against Terry's. She tried to ignore that she was lying in an enlarging pool of blood.

She used the sights to survey the flatlands. The natives had moved into a defensive formation, the soldiers in the back still shooting high in the sky at the disappearing satellite while those in front now aimed at the nests. Many of the nests had opened fire, several reporting someone hit by an arrow. She could hear Sgt. White's voice over the comlink giving orders to hold and force a retreat.

"Ames, why isn't your gun going? You jammed?"

"N-no, sorry, I—"

"Get it going!"

She tried to say something but just choked herself. Shifting the gun, she took aim at one of the great beasts and fired. Her shot hit the side of its shell, and it reared up. The rider screamed in pain, the shot piercing and burning the back of its leg. They tumbled as the beast lost its balance.

Elena felt sick, and she was mad at herself for it. So much training, so much big talk, and she turned out to be squeamish? Unacceptable.

She aimed again, put a native in her sights this time. Elena closed her eyes. Squeezed.

Even though she clung to the gun, it sent rivulets of shock through her whole body, making her toes shake. Her eye cracked open. The native lay face up across the back of its dazed beast.

She tried to swallow but her throat wouldn't work.

**6**

Taking a deep breath, Zeneba tried to focus her mind. It was the only way, Elder Zhora always said, to communicate with Nahara and Undin. If she was quiet, peaceful, completely focused, they would whisper in her ear and tell her the wonders of the world.

She tried desperately to hear their voices in the soft lulling breeze that gently brushed her cheek. The rustling leaves almost sounded like voices, but she could not understand what they said.

Cracking an eye open, Zeneba was utterly envious of Elder Zhora, sitting before her. Statuesque, the Skywatcher's sightless eyes were closed, his face relaxed, making his many wrinkles soften into small, almost smooth lines. She had asked him to teach her to commune with the Sunned Ones: She had thought that a leader should try to have direct contact with the divine. He heartily agreed, though he had been right to warn her that mastering such a skill as listening would be very difficult.

This all feeling very reminiscent of her struggle to master the *harn-da*, the skin-changing, Zeneba let out a small sigh.

There was no better place to try and speak with the Sunned Ones than in the Cloud Gardens. Attached to the top dome of Karak, the gardens seemed to touch the sky itself, the realm of the divine. Yet her old trouble plagued her; she couldn't quiet her mind. It was even worse now that she was *mara*—there was just too much to occupy her thoughts.

"They are coming," said Elder Zhora suddenly.

Zeneba's attention snapped to him. "What, Skywatcher?"

"They have returned. They need to see you."

Jumping up, she managed to bow quickly and say, "Thank you, Elder," before padding down the steep steps. Her heart racing, she headed quickly for the palace gates, almost running along the colonnade. She slowed to a more dignified pace as she approached the great staircase leading up into the Red Hall.

There was already a group of Elders along the middle tier, and a few steps down Yaro stood with some of his captains and Zaynab.

They parted for her, and she arrived just in time to watch a group of ragged warriors making their way past the gates and up the staircase. Her breath caught in her throat at the sight of Ondra.

He led his outfit even though half his head was wrapped in great *neen* leaves. He carried his arm as if it gave him trouble, holding it close to his tarnished breastplate. Bruises darkened his gray skin, and his iridescent swirls were a disheartening grayish-green. She had to stop herself from reaching out to him when he stopped before her.

"Forgive me," he began.

"What's happened?" she asked.

Ondra took a deep breath. "They attacked us, Golden One. We were doing a patrol when something great and terrible was sent into the sky. We tried shooting it down so that it wouldn't offend the Sunned Ones, but our arrows couldn't reach it. When they saw what we were doing, they fired on us."

"These do not look like arrow wounds," noted Elder Vasya.

Ondra shook his head. "These weapons are terrible to behold. They are great and loud and they sting and snarl and burn. It tears holes in flesh, gaping holes that can't . . . "

He couldn't finish, and Zeneba didn't want him to. She tried not to shudder. All those who had heard Ondra's words were silent, their eyes distant.

Composing himself, Ondra looked up at her again. He seemed harder somehow, the lines of his face sharp edges. But his eyes were glassy.

"My men fought bravely, Golden One, and we're sorry for failing you. We couldn't hold the tundra. Their perimeter grows every day and we couldn't risk the weapons coming to the villages."

She took his wrist in her hand and shook her head quickly. "You haven't failed me, Ondra. Not at all. You've given too much for me."

The hardness of his face eased at her soft words.

"You and your men will see the finest healers—I'll make sure of that. You'll be well again in no time at all."

Ondra bowed to her. "Chieftain Ura wanted to speak with you, Golden One. He's just beyond the gates with his people."

She gave him a small smile, placing her hand gently on the unhurt side of his face. His eyes grew a little wider at the contact, and his skin rippled into a muted, bashful orange.

"Rest easy," she said.

Zeneba led a small party down the great steps to the gates. Many Charneki had ventured into the main street, looking up to the palace. There was a great crowd in front of the gates, Chieftain Ura at their head.

Holding a hand out, she beckoned him closer. He came quickly and bowed his forehead down onto her hand.

"Bless your name, Golden One."

"No, bless yours, Chieftain. You have suffered too much, and I am sorry for it."

"Forgive me for being presumptuous, Golden One, but I had no other choice. My people need sanctuary."

"Think no more on it," she said, sorry to see the deep lines of shame that creased his forehead. "You and your people will be welcome in Karak until their homes can be restored to them."

"Thank you, Golden One."

She tried to smile, to reassure, but her face just

wouldn't comply. When she looked about, she saw scared, uncertain faces. Her presence no longer assured her people, their worries too great.

Chieftain Ura's tundra people were especially downtrodden. Always known as a hearty, stubborn folk, the Charneki of the north wouldn't have abandoned their homes were it not for the greatest threat. To see such brave Charneki with ashen complexions shook Zeneba to her core.

"You all will be made comfortable in the Red City, but you won't have to stay long," she said, making her decision as she spoke. "Your homes shall be taken back, that I promise you. I'll see to it myself."

"Golden One, what are you saying?" asked Yaro, stepping forward.

"I've a mind to go to the tundra and see these demons. They have threatened my people, and this I do not take lightly."

"Surely someone should go in your stead," said Elder Vasya.

Zeneba couldn't contain her scowl. "You wanted action from me, Elder. Well now you have it. I must see for myself the danger. I must face what my people have faced. I will see what can be done about these demons."

Elder Vasya matched her scowl, but he said nothing.

"It will take time, Golden One," Yaro argued, "to raise an army."

"Fine. But I will go."

"I'm going too!" said Zaynab, pushing past Yaro.

"You certainly are not," said Zeneba and Yaro together.

"But I could be *useful*." He marched up to her. "You gave Ondra a chance to prove himself. Why can't I?"

Her mouth opened and closed several times, for she was unable to come up with a good counterargument. She glowered down at him.

"It's going to be dangerous—you saw what

happened to Ondra and his men. I don't want you getting hurt."

"I won't! I'll even let Yaro follow me around everywhere."

"Yaro will have better things to do."

"Let me help him do those things. I'm being trained, Zeneba. I can be something useful to you, if you'd only let me!"

He was giving her his best pout, coupled with a determined frown. It was an expression she had seen many a time and one she always weakened at.

Pointing one long finger at his nostrils, she growled, "If you make any kind of trouble, I'll send you back. Understand?"

He nodded smugly.

She continued to glare at him, thinking to herself she might just leave without him despite her promise, if only to punish him for making such a scene in front of Chieftain Ura and the Elders.

Saving face, she turned back to the Charneki gathered before her.

"I leave soon for the north to deal with these demons. I do not know yet what awaits me there, but this I promise you—I will fight to my last breath for you!"

There were cries of thanks and tears poured from some eyes. Their skin rippled from gray to a muted purple, the *mara*'s assurances giving them some heart.

Next she turned to the Elders standing behind her.

"Elders, my good council, I will leave you as stewards of my seat. Protect it well as I defend my people."

They bowed reverently as Zeneba, with an energized Zaynab bouncing behind her, climbed back up to the palace. Her head buzzed with ideas, and she had to think. She headed for the Cloud Gardens.

"What're you thinking?" Zaynab asked, following her up the stairs.

"I'm trying to think of a plan. They'll expect me to have one."

"And?"

Groaning, Zeneba sank down onto a step. She rested her head on a hand.

"That's not good," Zaynab said, plopping down beside her.

"I'm not sure I can have much of a plan—at least not yet," she said, more to herself than him, "for I don't know what the demons will do. Their weapons are a problem."

"An enemy's weapon is always a problem."

She nodded. "We will go with an army—not a big one, but something much larger than Ondra's outfit. We'll camp just south, and our show of numbers might make them think twice about anything. They are large in number, but nothing to us, and Ondra's scouts seemed to think that most weren't warriors. The advantage would be ours then. We might be able to pressure them into negotiation."

"You want to talk to them?"

She looked at him. His question wasn't incredulous or snide. He gazed up at her innocently, curiously.

"If I can."

"You think that could solve it?"

"I hope so. It's better than the alternative."

Zaynab sighed. "That's true."

She nudged his should with hers. "You think it will work?"

He grinned. "Of course. You're *mara*."

7

The place had an eerie quality about it, full of abandoned items and lives. From the things strewn about the houses, Elena could make small guesses about the former inhabitants; this one worked with their hands, this one wove, another was making some sort of food. That is, until they had left.

The report surprised them somewhat, that the natives had up and left the tundra region. Elena couldn't blame them—getting shot at wasn't something they would soon forget.

For now, it seemed the humans were alone in the north, with winter fast approaching. They hadn't been able to sow crops, the ground too cold with the coming winter—not to mention Dr. Oswald and the other scientists were beginning to think the ground might never thaw enough to support substantial enough crops.

To Elena that meant a future of tasteless protein packs.

To General Hammond it meant further expeditions south, pushing towards more fertile soil. The abandoned native village, she hoped, would reveal if that was far enough south, or if they would have to push even further.

"Look at this," Cass said, her voice barely more than a whisper.

Elena headed over, her crunching boots thunderous.

"They were making a meal—probably just sitting down to dinner before . . ."

Elena gripped Cass's elbow and drew her out of the house. Best not to think about it too much. That's what Elena tried to do—block it out. If she didn't, all she heard was gunshots.

"I'm sure they're fine," she found herself saying. They walked past rows and rows of domed houses. Most of them were comprised of only a few rooms, the main one the largest with tables, seats, cookware, tools, cloth, food, plants, and other assorted household items. Many seemed somewhat disheveled, as if the former occupants had had to decide what to take hastily before getting out.

Such a thing struck Elena as enormously sad. She didn't really have a home, at least not yet. Her barren apartment hardly counted. She barely had anything of her own anymore, the sparse luggage she had packed back on Earth now, for the most part, useless and too small. Having to leave would be easy; she would just get up and go. Nothing to decide on, nothing to worry about. And that was sad.

Cass crossed her arms over her chest. "This feels . . . wrong. You know?"

Elena just shook her head, urging them to catch up with the main party.

Dr. Oswald was walking briskly to the eastern side of the settlement, a determined look on his face. The soldiers were having a time keeping up with him.

"He's found something," Cass said, hurrying up.

The doctor stopped short of a great pit, peering down into what seemed like a dark, gaping mouth in the middle of the ground. Elena didn't like it and refused to get very close.

"Interesting," said the doctor.

"A waste pit?" Cass asked.

"No—better. A mine."

"A mine?" someone repeated.

"Yes."

"It makes sense," said another scientist; Elena thought her name was Nadine, "there are no farms around and very few workshops. They most likely had to make their livelihoods somehow, had to make something tradable. This has the look of a mine."

As Dr. Oswald began walking around the side of the hole, one of his aides asked, "What could they have been mining?"

"Let's find out."

Having discovered a staircase carved from the stone of the cave wall, Dr. Oswald nimbly hopped down the first few steps and descended into darkness. His gauntlet became a lantern of blue light, guiding his way down. The other scientists and aides followed him, along with some of the soldiers, though they grumbled about it.

Elena herself moved as slowly as she could towards the stairs. Cass looked over her shoulder to see Elena with a displeased, scrunched face.

"Oh, c'mon," she said, "it'll be fascinating! It might be a whole new element for all we know."

"Yeah, sure, great. Have fun. Knock yourself out."

Cass made a face. "C'mon, scaredy-cat. You wouldn't want me to think you're anything less than big and bad, right?"

About to be pushed into the mine, Elena jumped

onto the first step before she fell. Shooting a glare at Cass, she held her gun tight as they activated their gauntlets and headed down, down, down.

The team amassed at the beginning of a wide shaft. The scientists began taking ground samples, brushing away dirt, inspecting technique. The soldiers looked about warily. Elena shared their sentiment—who knew what could be down there with them.

The doctor gave a shout. "Well now! This is something—Cass look at this."

Cass leaned over his shoulder and read the findings on his gauntlet. "That chemical makeup looks a lot like . . . "

"Coal!" Holding up a jagged piece of blue rock for all to see, Dr. Oswald said, "These rocks could be some sort of fuel source for the natives, similar to coal back on Earth."

"Could we use them, perhaps? Take some of the strain off the generators?" asked Cass.

"We'll need to do more scans, but yes, that's my hope."

The science team was all smiles. They talked in science jargon, with elements and scientific names, all of which became white noise in Elena's ears. She was just happy to see Cass livening up.

When they were done collecting a hearty amount of samples, the team headed back up, Elena leading the way out of the dark hole. The years aboard ship had been time enough in enclosed spaces.

She breathed the fresh air happily.

Cass gently punched her arm. "There now—not so bad. Worth it!" She held up the blue rock in the sunlight.

It was actually a pretty thing, sapphire in color at its center. It was almost glassy, and she could just barely see Cass's face through the rock. She couldn't quite believe the thing would burn and produce energy, but that's why she was a soldier, not a scientist.

"Just think," Cass said, starting what Elena knew would be a long bout of science chatter, "if we're able to utilize these, we can produce energy with things from Terra Nova. Not from the ship, but here, our home. It's the first step towards sustainability, all in a little blue rock! This could mean expansion for plants, factories, homes . . . "

It wasn't that Elena minded Cass getting worked up about things she liked, but her attention flew to something purple and flapping out on the horizon. She stopped. Squinted. Other soldiers stopped and followed her gaze. One of them took out a pair of specs, but Elena didn't need them to know the natives had returned.

———————

Rhys knew he should be feeling guilty. He had done as promised for two months now, hadn't gone near the perimeter. He had been nice to Hugh, had done what he was told even if it made him sore to do it.

But that was before the report of the natives returning. The military was beside itself, extending the perimeter, digging more machine gun nests, and in general beefing up a defense that had already proven enough to keep native things out and humans in.

Rhys didn't mind. With all the hubbub, he found it easier than ever to slip past the defenses. He knew there was some irony there, but he was too excited to ponder on it. The extended perimeter was closer to a grove of tall trees, and while he was sure they would be cut down eventually, for now they served as very helpful ladders, and he was able to jump the perimeter his preferred way.

He landed softly and began the long walk towards the abandoned village. It wasn't common knowledge, but Rhys had learned from Hugh that a new fuel source had been discovered at the village and that was why the military wouldn't give it back without a fight. Rhys thought that was a stupid reason not to give them back their homes.

Even though Elena terrified him, he still made his way further and further from New Haven. Bearing southwest, he headed to where the flatland became craggy hills, all in an effort to spot a native again.

The glimpse he had gotten ignited the firestorm of his imagination. They weren't like the species from other planets in old Earth movies. There were no tentacles, no gaping mouths. From what he had seen, and what he could imagine, they were graceful, honorable, and none too pleased about suddenly having to share their planet.

Bouncing off rocks, Rhys kept to the low dips between the hills and boulders, sticking to shadows. It was a cold morning, and he pulled his coat around himself tighter. It was getting too small. Shoving his hands in his pockets to keep them from the biting air, he stalked down a dry creek bed.

From what he had caught of people talking and what Hugh would give up, the native encampment was southwest of the village, the party having stopped when they realized that the village had been taken. They had made camp, scanners said, and it looked as if they meant to stay for some time.

That was good for him—if they left too soon he might not get to see them.

Little bluish creatures slithered across his path, propelling themselves with small legs and long tails. He didn't worry about them too much; they had small teeth that weren't venomous.

What he did have to worry about were the ice-cats, as he called them. Big scaled beasts, they were actually quite amazing to behold, purplish skin shimmering, but their bite wasn't worth it. He had only seen a few and presumed they were solitary creatures, but they nonetheless stalked the tundra region. He didn't need one of those anywhere near him.

It was because he was thinking of the ice-cats' two rows of long, spear-like teeth that he stopped cold when he heard rocks sliding up ahead. His breath caught in his throat. The soft crunch of rock underfoot sent him sailing towards the nearest large boulder.

He could have kicked himself. He had followed the creek bed straight into a dry canyon. Well, canyon might have been an exaggeration, but the walls were just high enough that he couldn't jump for it and pull himself up and out. He was trapped.

Inching down, he pulled his pocketknife out of his boot and clicked it open. He wondered if anyone would make it to him if he yelled his head off. He could try and set off one of the perimeter alarms, but that was almost a click away.

The crunching was getting closer and his heart raced.

His knuckles white around the pocketknife, foolhardy bravery washed over him. Maybe if he brought Hugh the ice-cat's head, his brother would finally stop hovering.

He put his hand over his nose and mouth when he couldn't quiet his breathing. It was coming. So close.

His head snapped to the right when it came up alongside him, only a few steps away. His heart stopped. His eyes went wide.

A native, a young native, stared back at him, its

square, bluish-gray eyes wide with astonishment. Its colorful sections of skin rippled into a white, then a blue. It took a step back, its hairless brows rising and coming together. It murmured what sounded like words.

Rhys knew he should have been more worried, but he was too amazed to do anything. He took in the native with awe. It wasn't that tall, only a few inches taller than him, but was lithe; sinewy muscles ran up and down its narrow limbs. It wore a sort of skirt-like piece of clothing with a broad sash, a scabbard folded into it. Rings of gold and some green stone ran up and down its upper arms, and on its narrow chest were two red native handprints.

Slowly he pushed off from the boulder to stand straight and face the native. It watched him carefully, its eyes travelling to his hand with the pocketknife.

The native crouched down a little, shouted something, and its hand went for a long dagger at its side.

"No, no, it's fine!"

Rhys threw the pocketknife on the ground and put his hands up.

"See? It's fine, I don't mean any trouble."

The native regarded him warily, curiously, before straightening. It looked Rhys up and down, then at the pocketknife on the ground. It craned its long neck to one side, then the other, assessing how much of a threat he might be. Then it put the dagger back into the scabbard.

Rhys sucked in a breath.

"Well."

The two of them stood there staring at each other for a long moment.

Finally the native took a cautious step towards Rhys. He stood still, thinking to let it come to him, but in all honestly he was too much a bundle of nerves to do anything.

The native surveyed him and quickly touched the cloth of his jacket before retreating. It rubbed its smaller, thumb-like finger and one long one together and looked quizzically back at Rhys.

Thinking he understood, Rhys unzipped the jacket slowly and then slipped out of it. He held up the jacket, which the native took from him, holding it up to the light. It seemed to understand that the jacket was clothes and was quickly finished with it. It handed the jacket back.

What it was more interested in was the bared skin of Rhys's forearms. It came towards him, again slowly, its eyes wide as it considered his pinky flesh. Rhys held up his arm to it.

The native opened its mouth in what Rhys thought might be a smile. It had what looked like teeth, similar in shape and size to his own, but when he looked at them more, he realized that they were only two curved teeth, one on the top, one on the jaw, rather than a bunch of smaller individual ones.

The native held out its own forearm, showing off its grayish skin. There was a snaking line of iridescent skin on the top of its forearm, which rippled into a deep orange. Slowly, with a trembling finger, Rhys touched the colorful patch. It felt slightly different from the rest of the skin; where the latter was rather rough and coarse, the former was almost soft.

"*Harn-da*," said the native as its skin deepened into an even more brilliant orange.

Rhys looked up in amazement, and a grin broke out over his face.

"You can speak!" Holding out his own forearm, he pinched some flesh. "Skin."

The native nodded, seeming to understand.

They gazed at each other again, both suddenly giddy.

Rhys pointed up. "Sky."

"*Gandin.*"

Rhys repeated the native word, the sound feeling foreign and exciting in his mouth.

The rest of the morning was spent with the two pointing and naming. They discussed rocks, *yaza*, grass, *bahnin*, hands, *lomu*, clouds, *vandin*, and even ears. The native had no word for that, as it didn't have any, or at least no fleshy outer portion. It pointed to ear holes instead and called those *turra*.

A new world unfurled before Rhys that day. He stood on the edge of a language, a culture, a people that he knew only the tiniest fraction about. But he wanted to know more. Everything. He had to.

As the suns crossed the sky and began coming down, Rhys pointed them out and found they were named Nahara and Undin, Nahara being the full sun that Terra Nova orbited and Undin the smaller, more distant one that was currently more than half hidden by the other sun. The native said more words about them, but he didn't catch anything. What he could say was that the native seemed to like them.

Realizing the time, Rhys stood and stretched out his cramping legs. The rocky ground hadn't been comfortable to sit on for so long, but he only noticed when he stood.

Pointing in the direction of home, he said, "That's the colony. It's our city. They're calling it New Haven."

The native looked a little confused.

Rhys pointed again. "New Haven."

The native repeated the words, its 'n' hard and his 'a' very drawn out. Its mouth moved a little uncomfortably to form the unfamiliar sounds. Rhys nodded and the native smiled and stood up. It pointed further south.

"Karak."

Rhys repeated the word, though he couldn't guess if that was the word for home or perhaps the village the native was from.

The native said quite a few words, none of which Rhys could catch, as it rearranged the dagger in its sash. Rhys picked up his pocketknife.

They looked at each other and grinned.

Rhys pointed at the ground. "Here again?"

The native shook his head, not understanding.

Rhys gestured towards New Haven and to Karak

and then brought his fingers together and pointed them down.

"Meet again here?"

Its eyes widened and it nodded enthusiastically. Pointing at the suns, it made two wide circles.

He had to think for a minute. "Meet again in two days?" He held up two fingers, repeated the circles, and pointed at the ground again.

The native nodded and made a whooping sound.

"Awesome! I'll see you then—oh." Straightening, Rhys waved his hand slowly. "Good-bye."

Grinning, the native did a little bow. "*Hunar een ua.*"

Rhys bowed and repeated the phrase as best he could while the native waved good-bye to him.

They turned to leave each other, when Rhys realized something.

"Oh, hey! Hey!"

The native stopped and looked at him.

"I didn't get your name." He pointed at himself. "Rhys."

The native pointed at him too. "Rhys." It sounded more like 'rice' than 'Rhys,' but he smiled nonetheless to hear it say his name.

Smiling too, the native pointed at its own chest. "Zaynab."

---

Zeneba entered the billowing tent to find it already filled with her captains.

"Golden One," they said when they saw her, bowing.

"Let us begin," she said.

She walked up to the long table that had been set in the middle of the tent and took a seat in the high-backed chair standing at the center. There were many dried *ronta* leaves strewn over the table, used as scrolls and maps. They were already covered in glyphs and other markings; she recognized at least one battle stratagem.

"We know for certain that their southern

borders are well protected, especially close to their city," said Chieftain Ura.

"And what of their northern border?" asked Yaro.

"We haven't made it that far yet—their patrols are constant and their defenses continue to stretch outward. If we were to attack the city, from the north would perhaps be best, provided we can make it around the southern defenses."

"Let us worry about reclaiming the village first," said Zeneba. "I promised your people their homes back, Chieftain. I'd rather not give them a war instead."

"That might prove too naïve of a plan, Golden One," said Elder Vasya. "To attack them may be the only way to reclaim the tundra."

Zeneba tried not to grimace. Elder Vasya had travelled all the way north with them to continue being a naysayer. She had wanted to make him stay in Karak, but the council had insisted it would be good to have at least one Elder with her.

"We would be attacking blind, Wise One," Yaro offered, sensing Zeneba's frustration.

"Further scouting is needed," said another captain, Samuka, "before any idea of attack."

"Well yes, of course," Elder Vasya conceded, "but an attack we need nonetheless."

"I will *not* have war, Elder, not if I can help it," said Zeneba.

"You already have one, *mara*."

The tent descended into uncomfortable silence as both Zeneba and Elder Vasya glared straight ahead instead of at each other.

"Though I have brought an army, I hope to use it to make peace, not war."

"The demons certainly will not see the diplomacy in your army. Your plan is short-sighted."

Her eyes widened at the insult. She hadn't been talked to like that since her minority, and she didn't much like it then either.

"You are dismissed, Wise One," she said.

All looked at her in surprise.

Elder Vasya turned a livid face to her. "I am not one of your captains, Golden One. I am an erudite member of the Elders, wise, all-seeing. I am not yours to dismiss."

"Then I would ask you to leave."

His eyes narrowed. "We, the Elders, choose the *mar*. We divine who will lead all Charneki. We chose you—we *made* you."

Yaro straightened to his full height and took a small step forward, putting himself between the Elder and Zeneba.

"Are you threatening the *mara*, Elder?"

Elder Vasya straightened too. "Of course not, captain. I am only reminding the *mara* to show a little respect."

They continued to glower at one another as the other captains, after a few more tense moments, tried to carry on. Yaro remained rooted to Zeneba's side.

"Their defenses are strong around their city, but not as much so around the village. The demons have claimed the village, as we knew, but it doesn't look like they inhabit it yet," said Ondra.

"Why are they interested in our village?" she asked.

"We believe they've found the *buna* mines," answered Chieftain Ura.

"A fuel source such as the mines would ensure their staying," said Elder Vasya.

Shifting, Chieftain Ura replied, "Yes, it could mean that."

"This does not change the plan," insisted Zeneba. "We must still reclaim the village and secure it—before their defenses are bolstered."

"What would you have us do, Golden One?" said Chieftain Ura.

She bit her lip a moment before saying, "Continue scouting—see how far north you can push. This may become useful. But our main efforts should be in understanding the situation at the village—how many soldiers, how powerful, any weaknesses. When we are ready, we will reclaim and secure the village."

"And then?" asked Elder Vasya.

"Then, once the fighting has stopped, we will see if these demons can be reasoned with. Our superior numbers should discourage them from wanting further conflict."

The Elder held in a scoff. "What if the fighting does not stop?"

"We'll secure the village, Golden One, you have our word," said Ondra quickly, looking between her and the Elder.

Her face softened momentarily to give him a grateful nod.

"I have every faith. May the Sunned Ones bless us."

With that the captains bowed and exited, Elder Vasya trailing sulkily behind them.

"He is very . . . disagreeable of late," said Yaro.

"I think he's always been like that," said Zeneba, rubbing her closed eyes. "Yaro, do you . . . do you think he means anything by it?"

"He is a Wise One."

"That's not an answer."

Yaro opened his mouth but closed it again. "Whatever happens, I will protect you. You need not fear him. Or anyone."

She gave him a small smile. "I know, Yaro. Thank you. Don't let me keep you—I'm just tired is all."

Yaro bowed to her, though he still looked concerned. He left her in an empty, silent tent.

She took the rare occasion to think. Sometimes she went days without hearing her own thoughts. How could she be expected to say her opinion, give orders, when she couldn't find her own voice in all the noise?

Though she hated to think on it, Elder Vasya's warmongering opinions were beginning to take root in her mind. She loathed the idea of sending Charneki into battle, and, to make things worse, she knew very little of war. Yaro had taught her the warrior's way, but being able to wield sword, spear, and shield were far different from leading her warriors into battle and possibly death. The thought weighed heavily upon her mind.

She chose to believe there was another solution. Focusing all her energy on reclaiming the village kept her from having to consider the sharpening reality of war. She also liked to think that their superior numbers would mean something—she certainly wouldn't want to send her warriors against such a numerous foe.

Zeneba saw something moving at the mouth of the tent from the corner of her eye. She looked over to see Zaynab poking his head through.

"Can I come in?"

She grinned, the sight of her brother momentarily alleviating her mind of such somber thoughts. She was almost happy he had come along.

"Of course."

He sauntered in, his hands behind his back. He looked about to make sure they were alone before coming to her and saying, "You look terrible."

She laughed. "Well thank you. That helps."

He wandered around the table, inspecting the papers.

"So what's the plan?"

"Reclaim what's ours."

He nodded, though it seemed absentminded. Poring over a map, he traced a finger around the region that the demons now held.

She watched him for a long while, wondering what thoughts were whirring through his head. She said his name several times, but he seemed unable to hear her.

"How can we know?" he said suddenly.

"What now?"

"How can we know if they really are demons?"

He looked up from the map when she didn't answer. Her mouth was open, yet nothing came out. She truthfully couldn't answer him. Rubbing her heavy forehead, the question threatened to overwhelm her.

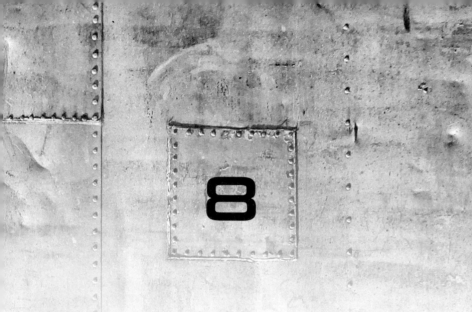

**8**

Rhys skidded through the dry creek bed, overturning rocks in his hastiness.

He found his friend already there and with company. Rhys came to a quick stop to marvel at the big animal. He had seen one before—the warriors rode them, great turtle-like beasts with spiked tails.

"Hey!" he said.

Zaynab looked up. "*Yan amar*, Rhys."

He did a low whistle. "Who's this?" He pointed at the turtle-creature.

"He is *garan*," Zaynab said.

Rhys smiled and nodded at the use of English.

The two of them were picking up the other's language fairly well. Rhys liked languages and learning them—back on Earth he had been fluent in Canto and Hindi, both good for talking on the busy city streets. He was out of practice with them now, but he was happy to make room for this new Charneki language.

"Is *garan* his name?"

Zaynab shook his head. "He is called Barrah."

"Is he yours?"

Zaynab frowned, not understanding.

Rhys pointed from the *garan* to Zaynab. "Yours?" When he still seemed unsure, Rhys tried making the motion of riding. "You ride him?"

He smiled and nodded. "Yes. I am *unhar*. *Unhar* ride *garan*."

Zaynab made a motion and Rhys walked up slowly to the animal. It regarded him rather apathetically and didn't move as he reached out a hand to touch its head. Its scaly neck and head were rough and coarse, but its beaked mouth was smooth. He seemed smaller than the other *garans* Rhys had seen, but then, Zaynab was smaller than the other warriors.

"Why a warrior, Zaynab?" he asked.

He shook his head.

"You a warrior?" he tried.

His expression must have been quizzical enough that Zaynab understood the question.

Zaynab thought for a moment, trying to find a word that they could both understand.

"*Preuria*," he said.

Rhys shook his head.

Zaynab thought again. Finally he put his arms together in front of his face and repeated, "*Preuria*."

Rhys still didn't understand.

Zaynab seemed frustrated and looked about. Suddenly his eyes were wide, and he pounced on his *garan*. From its back he took up a great circular shield. Holding it up proudly for Rhys, he said again, "*Preuria*."

"Shield," said Rhys.

Zaynab nodded, repeated the English word, and then put it down.

"*Preuria nahin-ira aue ya.*"

Rhys could only understand 'shield' and *ira*, 'my.'

Seeing he still didn't get all of it, Zaynab repeated, "*Nahin.*" He thought, then pointed at Rhys and then himself, "*Valar.*"

"Person?"

Zaynab frowned, seeming unsure if 'person' matched, and then pointed at the smaller sun.

"Undin. Undin is *valar*?"

Again he nodded. "*Undin bua-na valar.*" He pointed to the bigger sun. "*Nahara bua-ni valah.*"

"Nahara's a woman?"

Zaynab grinned encouragingly, pointing to Rhys, then himself, then Undin, and repeating, "*Valar.*"

"So Undin is a man and Nahara is a woman."

Zaynab grinned again.

"But what's that got to do with you being a warrior? Is Undin an *unhar*?"

Zaynab shook his head and took up the shield again. "*Preuria.*" He pointed at Nahara. "*Valah.*"

"So you . . . you're shielding a woman?"

He nodded enthusiastically.

"Oh! You're protecting someone! A woman? Who?"

"Zeneba."

"Who is Zeneba?"

"She is *nahin.*"

Rhys thought for a moment. "Sister? Is she your sister?"

Zaynab looked like he wanted to agree but was unsure.

Taking up two rocks, Rhys said, "*Yara,*" the Charneki word for mother, having learned it talking about Nahara. The other rocked he called "Father," and Zaynab nodded slowly. He put the rocks together and picked up another pair of rocks. "Children," he called them. He held out one rock, called it "Brother, *valar* child," and then held up the second rock and said, "Sister, *valah* child."

Zaynab was frowning but after a moment he nodded. "Sister," he said.

Hoping they meant the same thing, Rhys smiled. "So you are *unhar* to *preuria* your *nahin?*"

Happy with the words, Zaynab nodded.

"Is your *nahin* in Karak?" Rhys asked.

He shook his head. "Zeneba . . . " he searched for the words, and when he couldn't find them, said instead, "*Buran lahn preuria kallamar nua.*"

From what he could understand of that, Zeneba had come to protect the tundra.

"She's here?" He pointed at the ground.

Zaynab pointed off towards the Charneki encampment.

"Is she *unhar?*"

"She is *mara*," Zaynab said, a smile spreading across his face. His skin turned a golden hue at the word.

Rhys didn't know what *mara* meant, and

Zaynab couldn't quite find the words to explain it to him, but he at the very least understood that she was important.

Zaynab's mouth curved up impishly and Rhys saw the glint of an idea flash in his eyes. He pointed at his *garan*.

"Ride?"

Rhys's face lit up, and he nodded exuberantly.

Zaynab held onto some tethers and guided Rhys up onto the animal. It was higher than he thought and made him feel heady. Zaynab gave a command and the *garan* began to lumber forwards.

Rhys whooped in excitement as Zaynab jumped up behind him. They spent the rest of the afternoon goading Barrah to go faster, laughing every time the *garan* sped up and immediately slowed down again.

---

Groaning, Hugh clumsily reached over and tapped his gauntlet to turn off the chiming alarm. Rolling onto his back, he rubbed his eyes and for a few moments, let himself fantasize that it wasn't morning.

Finally he managed to roll out of bed. He changed into clothes quickly, the cold morning air making him even faster. Fastening his gauntlet, he walked out of his room.

The faint light of the dawn crept through the windows, making the walls of the apartment glow. He stepped into a shaft of light and stretched.

He was fishing around for his warmest jacket when he noticed Rhys's door was open. Straightening, he craned his neck to see Rhys's legs sprawled out on top of the bed.

Hugh hadn't heard Rhys come in the night before, and whatever he had been doing made him tired enough to forget to close his door, a rare thing. Hugh walked over to the open threshold and smirked to see Rhys hadn't even taken off his boots.

Tiptoeing into the room, Hugh gingerly untied

the boots and set them on the ground. He then nudged Rhys until he rolled over, freeing the tangle of blankets beneath him. Softly unfurling them, Hugh spread them all out over Rhys until he was a lump under a mound of blankets.

He couldn't stop himself from touching a gentle hand to Rhys's head. It was like looking in a mirror at his younger self. But then, Rhys had always had a fire in him that Hugh was envious of. It made his eyes bright, like blue flame. Hugh thought his own rather dull.

He strode back out of the room and closed the door behind him before his luck ran out.

Slipping his arms into his jacket, Hugh shut the front door behind him and headed for work.

Pushing the sleeve up above his gauntlet, Hugh typed in a command and then said into it, "Hey Rhys, you can take the day off, okay? You looked tired so go ahead and sleep in. If you could, though, would you run down to the store for me and get ten more protein packs? Don't forget to have it marked in the ration-book this time. Thanks, and I'll see you later."

He pushed a button and sent the voice message. Rhys would get it on his reader when he woke up.

Hugh had been giving Rhys a lot of days off, but that was mostly because it seemed to improve his mood. Rhys had been particularly well-behaved lately—though Hugh did wonder about it, especially when Rhys got in late. He rarely offered where he was going or had been. Hugh was beginning to suspect something must have happened. He loved his brother, but he knew better than to believe Rhys had suddenly come around.

He stopped when he saw the mass of people sitting outside the general's headquarters. He walked past the buildings every day on his way to the power plant, but had never seen such a crowd of people. From the looks of their heavy jackets and stiff movements, they had camped out there all night.

His walk was slowed as he hit the back lines of

people. He quietly maneuvered past them on his way towards the plant and was confounded by all the dirty looks he received.

"Still here I see."

Hugh turned, recognizing the general's voice. Those who had been sitting stood quickly, everyone looking at General Hammond standing in the open door.

"We should be able to talk with you when we have concerns," Hugh heard a man say who was close to the general. "We're part of this colony, too."

"I've already addressed your concerns, Carter," said the general, her voice as icy as the morning air.

"That's a lie."

The general folded her hands behind her back.

"Are you calling me a liar?"

The crowd shifted anxiously.

"I'm saying you don't follow through. You say

a lot of things, you promise us equality, but we never see any it," said the man, Carter.

"That sounds an awful lot like dissent."

"I'm not one of your soldiers, general! None of us are! We're concerned *citizens* of this colony who want our voices heard."

"I've told you once and I'll tell you again: democracy failed." She looked sharply out at the crowd gathered around. "Need I remind you of the fantastic failure democracy proved to be in the Last World War? Citizens didn't know what was needed and only made everything worse."

"We aren't at war!" exclaimed Carter.

"Wrong again. We *are* at war. The native threat is very real. In case you've forgotten, there's an army camped just five clicks from where we stand now. They have no interest in negotiating or hearing us out. They mean to drive us from here, and we haven't got anywhere else to go."

"We don't know what the natives want—have we even tried making peaceful contact with them?"

"I'll not risk the success of this colony over diplomatic quibbling. We are the vanguard of humanity's last hope. If we fail, humanity ends. Let me do my job and defend our new home and then we can think of such niceties as democracy and equality. Until then, get back to your homes."

Carter's mouth was agape as the door slammed in his face. The crowd immediately broke out in an excited, aggravated hum.

Stepping to the head of the crowd, Carter called for silence. He was a tall man, his shoulders broad and his dark skin pockmarked.

"I suppose we shouldn't have expected any better," he said, the crowd voicing loud agreements. "We can't wait for *her* to give up power. We'll all be dead and gone before that happens."

"The natives are just an excuse!" someone said.

"Yes, and when they're dealt with, there'll be another. It won't stop. If we want change, we have to start taking things into our own hands! We have to—"

A loud burst of gunfire ripped through the cold sky and everyone went silent. From the back of the headquarters a squadron of soldiers in full uniform and armor came to take position.

"She's set her dogs on us," Carter said before receiving the butt of a rifle to his face.

The wind was knocked out of Hugh as those around him began scattering, the soldiers starting to push the crowd away from the headquarters. Those closest to the buildings were receiving harsh punishment, shouldering blow after blow. Shots rang out into the sky.

His eyes, wide and blinking, couldn't make the sight of beaten bodies go away. He turned and ran.

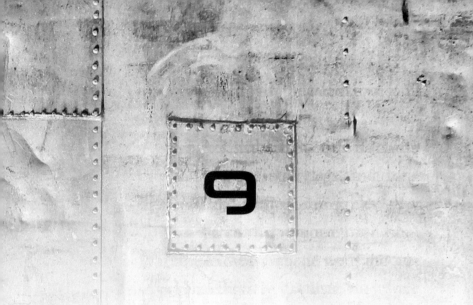

**9**

**C***lick*. Rhys brought the reader down to look at after the fake sound of camera shutters. Swiping right, he looked at the picture then showed Zaynab.

Zaynab marveled at the sight. He quite liked readers, especially taking pictures. The first time Rhys had brought one, he let Zaynab hold it. The Charneki had held it every which way, trying to figure out where the image came from. He seemed to understand now, after a lot of pictures taken, that they were made and stored in the little device.

Rhys liked the picture he had just taken, a

simple one of him and Zaynab smiling up into the reader's camera.

"I have something for you," Rhys said, and Zaynab looked up.

Reaching into his pack, Rhys took out another reader. It was actually Hugh's, but he never used it, preferring his gauntlet. He didn't feel too guilty about the theft as he watched Zaynab's face light up in a smile.

Zaynab took up the device gently, turning it about in his hands. He swiped a finger across the screen and looked delighted to see the pictures Rhys had already taken on the screen.

"How?" he asked, holding up the reader.

Rhys took it for a minute and showed him what to press and how to hold it.

"And then smile," he said, and the reader clicked again.

Zaynab took up the reader and tried himself. Soon he was turning in circles, taking pictures of everything.

"Picture!" he said gleefully. He turned and took one of Rhys while he made a face, and the two of them laughed.

Zaynab's eyes went wide, and he carefully placed the reader in one of his saddlebags. He then slid one of his green stone bracelets off his arm. He gestured and Rhys took off his heavy jacket so that Zaynab could slip the circle of stone up his arm. Though he was taller, Zaynab was much slimmer and the bracelet only went to Rhys's mid-forearm.

Zaynab smiled to see him wearing it. "*Uria sua ya*," he said, touching the circlet. "You Charneki now."

Rhys didn't quite know why his heart swelled to hear Zaynab say that.

The two smiled and sat down to inspect their gifts. Zaynab played with swiping and pressing as Rhys turned the green circlet around in his hands. There was a short inscription carved along the face, and it was fascinating for him to see the Charneki language written out. He was curious about the stone itself, too. He didn't know if Earth had anything like it—if it did, he hadn't heard of it. He resolved to head to the Central Intelligence Center, CIC, or what the military was calling the library, to find out.

"Rhys," said Zaynab after a while, "why Charnek? Why humans come to Charnek?"

"We needed a new home," he said.

"No home?"

He shook his head. Asking for Zaynab's reader, he pulled up a picture of Earth from six hundred years ago, back when it was still green and blue.

"Home?"

"Yeah. We called it Earth."

He swiped a finger across the reader and brought up another picture, one much more recent. The oceans were dark with run-off and the land was scarred and barren looking, all a muted dust color.

"This is Earth now."

Zaynab frowned. He opened his mouth and

made a motion with his finger, unable to find the words to ask what had happened.

"We were bad to our home. We couldn't live there anymore."

"Home dead?"

Rhys's gaze fell to the pebbly ground. "Yeah."

He didn't know why he was suddenly overcome. He had barely thought about Earth since waking up—there was too much to do and learn. But now, talking about it made him remember all that he had left behind. His mother's face, kind and sun-burned, made his heart ache.

He felt Zaynab's hand on his shoulder and looked up to find his friend with sympathetic eyes. He let Zaynab console him, feeling better as he touched the cool stone of the circlet.

"Home here," Zaynab said.

Rhys pawed at one of his eyes. "But it's your home already."

"Ground for humans," he said, "and ground for Charneki. Ground is big."

"You think there's ground for all of us?"

Zaynab nodded.

He was touched that Zaynab would welcome him, all the humans. They certainly hadn't given him a reason to welcome them, and it made Rhys hate the military regime and General Hammond even more. She was wrong about the natives. Every time she talked about the campaign against them she lied. The natives didn't want to drive them out or kill them all. They could be reasoned with. If some humans and some Charneki could get together and talk like he and Zaynab did, they might actually get somewhere.

"Stars carry you here?" Zaynab asked.

Rhys had to think a moment. "What do you . . . oh, the ships! Yes, we rode stars to come here."

"Did you ride far?"

"Yes, very far. Earth is very far away."

"You not go back?"

Rhys shook his head. "No. We can't."

He smiled. "Good—you stay."

Rhys's smile was only halfway done when it suddenly fell, a far off popping sound echoing through the creek bed.

Zaynab had gone still at the noise. He muttered something under his breath.

"Those are gunshots," Rhys murmured.

They didn't need to translate for each other that fighting had broken out.

———

Zeneba dashed from her tent to the sound of fighting. As a warrior came running up to her she demanded, "What's happened?"

"They are firing on us, Golden One—our scouts were seen."

Letting out a curse she had heard Yaro say more than once, and ignoring the warrior's obvious surprise, Zeneba headed into the chaotic camp, seeking out one of her captains. She came upon Chieftain Ura first.

"Golden One."

"What must be done?"

"They are pursuing our scouts back this way—we must prepare our defenses."

"See to it then, and please report to me when you can."

He made to leave her, but she stopped him with, "And Chieftain?"

"Yes, Golden One?"

"Let us defend ourselves, but do not fire on the demons."

She could tell he didn't like that order, his lips twitching.

"At least until we see what they do. If they attack, fire at will, but wait for them to make a move. I still have hope we might solve this without further bloodshed."

He bowed to her, and with that Chieftain Ura gathered the nearest warriors and headed north of the encampment to the battlements they had made while there.

Something off to her left caught her attention, and she watched as the scouting party came as quickly as the *garans* could lumber with armed demons not far behind. She could hear Chieftain Ura shouting orders to let them in and make ready.

Zeneba held her breath as she watched the warriors make it to the battlements and quickly get down. Archers were itching to notch arrows, but the Chieftain held his hand up in a fist, ordering them to wait.

"What is going on?" asked Elder Vasya, appearing beside her. "Why are they not attacking?"

"We shall see what these demons do first."

He turned quickly, no doubt disliking what she said, but she preempted him.

"Please, Wise One, apply your art to the scouts. Some of them might be in need of a healer."

He gave her an irritated scowl before moving off. He was slow to make his way down to the battle line, his eyes transfixed on the scene playing out before them.

Both sides, the Charneki and the demons, had taken up positions along a line of defensible terrain. The Charneki were dug in, mounds of upturned earth providing some shelter, yet while the demon warriors stood unprotected, their weapons, aimed at the Charneki line, threatened to prove defense enough.

Zeneba tried to swallow but found the lump in her throat prevented her. She stood on the crest of the tallest hill they had claimed for the camp, looking down on the whole scene. She trusted the bravery of her warriors, but she was breathless at the sight of so many demon warriors, even though the Charneki were tenfold greater in number.

They were odd looking to say the least. Covered from neck to toe in what looked like clothes, they stood quite shorter than a Charneki. Their bodies were stocky, broad, and they looked wholly ungraceful. Their skin ranged in color from pinky to brown, and most of them had hairs growing from their heads, several of what seemed like the males even having some on their faces. She thought them quite ugly.

Both sides continued to stare at each other, waiting for the other to move.

It was during that eerie silence that Zeneba suddenly felt cold on one side. She looked about, searching for the source. With a pang she realized it—she hadn't seen Zaynab all day.

"Yaro!" she cried, finding him in the line the Guards had made a few paces from her, ready to defend her should the need arise.

He looked over his shoulder and, at her gesture, came quickly.

"Where's Zaynab? Have you seen him?"

Yaro's skin faltered from a courageous red to a worried green.

"I believed him to be with you."

"Find him, Yaro, please!"

He was away from her in an instant, heading down the southwestern side of the hill. Zaynab had become fond of riding out that way, amongst the craggy hills and dry creek beds. She prayed to Nahara and Undin that he would be there, riding his *garan*. She couldn't bear to think of him being found by the demons.

Her worry over Zaynab and the very present threat of a demon attack fought for her attention so that she couldn't entirely focus on either. Her mind was awash in unintelligible worries, making her head heavy. She couldn't sort one thought from another as she stood by herself.

Her breath came in quick little breaths, and she knew she was on the precipice of losing the battle against her nerves. She fought and persevered for the present, telling herself to be brave like her warriors.

Ondra was glancing at her over his shoulder. He would have rushed to her. She gave him a quick shake of her head, telling him to stay in place and mind his post.

The small movement recovered some of her wits, and she took a deep breath, filling her lungs,

168

determined to get a grip on herself. She was *mara*. They needed her to be *mara*.

The stalemate persisted, neither side willing to be the aggressor. Zeneba couldn't tell if this was good or not; waiting on the edge of a battle seemed to be worse than anything after. She could see in the tense muscles of the warriors' shoulders that the inaction was taking its toll.

She tried to make her mind formulate a plan in case fighting did break out. It was hard, and she strained, but as she looked down along the dip of the hills, she determined that should they be pushed back, the high point would be where the warriors could launch a volley at the demons. They would hold the crest, where she stood, and advance from there.

Her thoughts were interrupted by Yaro calling from behind her, "Golden One!"

She turned to find him and Zaynab striding quickly up the slope. Going through a flurry of emotions at seeing Zaynab unharmed and impenitent, she drew him to her in a fierce embrace before scolding him.

"Where have you been?"

He shrugged. "Just riding. What have I missed?"

She didn't let him crane his head around her.

"I have enough to worry about without you going missing," she snapped.

He sated her anger a little by finally flushing with guilt. "I'm sorry—I lost track of the time. I was headed back when Yaro found me, right?"

He looked up to Yaro for aid but found little. The warrior had no doubt harbored his fair share of grief upon realizing Zaynab was missing on the eve of battle, for he was almost as fond of Zaynab as Zeneba was, though he rarely admitted it.

Yaro replied by retaking his position in the defensive line. He took with him a dirty look from Zaynab.

"I've a mind to send you home," she said.

His eyes grew wide with horror at that. "No, don't! I won't get lost again!"

Knowing there was something he wasn't telling her, she resolved, for the moment, to stay in the dark. Though she relieved some of her anxiety by saying, "Yaro will see to that. I wanted to put my Head to better use, but I see he must watch after you."

Zaynab took this news with as much enthusiasm as he did the prospect of being sent back to Karak.

"I'm not a *mahar* anymore—I don't need watching."

"Apparently you do. A *valar* would know better than to wander at a time like this! I thought you wanted to be *unhar*—you would so quickly abandon your post?"

He stared pointedly down at the ground during her speech, his guilt turning him a bluish-green. She could see the truth of it was affecting him, yet he remained obstinate, and she was left to think it must have something to do with what he wasn't telling her.

Her gaze went back to the stand-off below once

more now that her other worry was alleviated. Little had changed. Her warriors and the demons were shifting now and again, still waiting. She herself was almost tricked into wanting something to happen.

"What's happened?" asked Zaynab, coming to stand beside her.

She looked down at him, surprised at his low, almost sad tone. She wanted to snap at him to go into the tent and stay there, but she found the comfort he brought her, standing beside her, outweighed her will to punish him. Instead she wrapped an arm around his shoulders and held him against her.

They watched the scene below together in silence, which puzzled Zeneba. She had expected at least some small words from Zaynab upon seeing the battle. He seemed wholly devoid of his former desire for battle, and as she peered down at him, she thought him changed somehow.

"This doesn't have to happen," he said finally as Nahara and Undin began to wane.

"With some luck it won't."

He voiced no response, and she had the feeling she had misunderstood him.

As it were, little came of the stand-off besides frazzled nerves, and the would-be combatants finally retreated from the battle lines as darkness spread inky fingers out over the hills. Zeneba knew she should feel blessed, but she couldn't shake the feeling that the day had had a sense of portent.

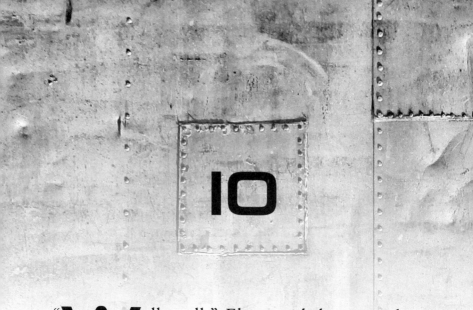

**10**

"**W**ell, well," Elena said, hopping down off the hood of the speeder, "I didn't expect it to be you two."

Hugh grinned. "Saranov could spare us today. So your engine's having trouble?"

"Seems to be—at least, that's what I think it is. But that's why you're the engineer."

"Let's take a look."

Heading over to the speeder, Hugh made quick work of opening it up and beginning to tinker. Elena found herself with a small smile watching him work, a determined frown adorning his face.

"So how're things?" Elena asked, looking down at a rather bored Rhys.

He looked up at her. They both knew what she meant.

"Fine," he said. "Just fine."

"What've you been getting up to?"

He gave her a sidelong glare. "Nothing."

He was a terrible liar, but Elena didn't want to call him on it in front of Hugh. She shifted her weight and continued to stare down at him, hoping to at least make him feel guilty for whatever it was he had done. He just crossed his arms and looked anywhere else.

They stood like that for some time with the sound of Hugh rifling around under the hood in the background.

Rhys opened his mouth, frowned, wrinkled his nose, and looked up at her.

"Has there been any word?" he asked. "About the natives, I mean."

She decided to play along.

"What kind of word?"

He gave her a look. "Like have they decided what they're going to do?"

"Nothing's official yet," she lied.

"But there's a plan?"

"It's safe to say that's confidential. You're a civilian, I can't—"

"Yeah. Right. Fine."

He went back to scowling with his arms crossed.

Elena regarded him curiously. Why in the world did he want to know? She was beginning to think it had something to do with what he had been up to when Hugh stood up, wiping his blackened hands on a rag.

"It looks like some of your tubes are shot. They'll need replacing."

"Okay—I think there's some replacement stuff over—"

"Nah, we can use extra ones from the engines."

"Like the *ship* engines?"

Hugh shrugged. "Yeah. They actually aren't

that much bigger and they'll give you less grief in the long run. We've been phasing out of using them during the switch to generators, so we have a bunch of extras."

She put her hands up. "Do what must be done; you're the expert."

Grinning, he said, "Rhys, would you mind running back to the plant and grabbing some while I get started? They're in the—"

But Rhys was already walking away. He waved at Hugh over his shoulder. "I know where they are," he said, stalking out of the hangar.

"Just a little ray of sunshine, that one," she said once Rhys had disappeared.

"He just doesn't like coming to work, that's all."

"I don't think I've ever seen him smile."

"He does." Hugh didn't sound that convincing. He saved face by grinning and looking over at her. "And I could say the same thing about you."

Giving his shoulder a punch, she said, "Yeah, yeah. Back to work."

Hugh got to work taking the old tubes out, and Elena plopped down onto a wheeled stool. She didn't mind the upgrade to her speeder at all—she was getting particularly fond of it, and anything that made it run better longer sounded good to her. She was always amazed when Hugh and Cass started spouting jargon. Sometimes it made her feel rather stupid. But she contented herself by thinking there was no one, save Sgt. White, who knew more about semi-automatics.

She watched his shoulders move this way and that, his head hidden behind them as he leaned over the hood. Soon she was propelling herself around on the stool by shoving herself off.

"I smile," she found herself saying.

"Hmm?" Hugh looked up. His face already had a few streaks of grease on it.

"I said I do smile."

He chuckled. "No you don't."

"Yes, I do. Look."

She stretched her lips over her teeth.

He gave her a horrified look. "What is *that*?"

She glared but held the smile. "I'm smiling."

"That's not what it's called."

After giving him a sour look, Elena resumed pushing herself around on the stool.

Glancing over his shoulder at her, Hugh broke out into a grin. "Okay, fine, you smile. It's pretty rare, though. But when you do, it's nice."

"Yeah?" she said, spinning around to face him.

His eyes went a little wider and he blushed. "Y-yeah," he said and returned to his work.

She watched him for a while, wondering what that had been about. Hugh could be weird around her sometimes, especially if it was just the two of them without Cass.

Catching her watching him, Hugh cleared his throat.

"Has work been harder lately?" he asked.

She shrugged. "It's been longer."

"Is something going to happen?"

Meeting his gaze, she nodded slowly. They had

never had secrets before, and she didn't like that they needed to now with their jobs. She looked around, making sure the hangar was clear. Hugh knowing wasn't going to change the plan.

"Yeah. The general wants the natives out of the tundra. We're going to flush them out."

Hugh stopped and straightened. He was looking at her in a way she couldn't describe.

"You'll be on that detail?"

She couldn't tell him, couldn't make her mouth form the words to say how much she didn't want to go. It wasn't that she disliked soldiering—she felt she was actually quite good at it—but the idea of killing the natives made her stomach feel like it was tied all up in knots. She knew they were a threat, that they had to be moved away, but she didn't have to like the military's method.

It didn't seem fair. She could still see it as vividly as the day she did it, shooting that native warrior, watching its limp body sprawled across its beast's back. It hadn't seen it coming, hadn't even seen her. It wasn't fair, squatting in that camouflaged hole, sniping them with primitive weapons. They hadn't a hope of defending themselves, not for long at least.

"Yeah."

"You . . . " He looked down at his hands, holding a grimy rag. "You'll be careful. Right?"

"Always am."

He nodded, still looking at the ground. "Good. I-I wouldn't . . . I wouldn't want anything to happen to you."

She was stunned into silence at that and could only watch him return to work. No response came to her, so she just sat there. He had never said anything like that before, and it wasn't like the mission would be different than any other. Well, they would be on the offensive for once, and while human soldiers were greatly outnumbered by native warriors, Elena had absolute faith in their technological advantage. Again, no defense of the natives' would hold for long.

Hugh cleared his throat again. "How soon?"

"Tonight."

"Really?"

She nodded. "Yup. We're ordered to kill as few as possible, but the goal is to flush them out. Hopefully they get the message pretty quick. They should—"

"You can't!"

Hugh and Elena jumped, startled to see Rhys standing not far away, the tubes Hugh needed clutched in his white, shaking fist. He was glaring at Elena, his eyes glinting with hot, angry tears.

"You can't just do that to them!"

Turning to him, Elena said, "We have to secure our—"

"*No*! This isn't even our land! We took it from them, just came here and stole it. It's not ours—they're just trying to get back their homes! And you're going to kill them for it!"

"It's our home now too, Rhys," Hugh tried, his voice soft. "We have to try and defend it."

"They're not attacking us! You don't know them—they wouldn't hurt us. It's us that's attacking *them*! They're just defending themselves. It's us that's the problem!"

"Rhys, I know you—"

"No! You don't know anything! You're just going to stand by and let them get murdered! And you!" He turned on Elena, pointing an accusing finger. "You're going to murder them!"

Throwing the tubes down on the ground, Rhys ran from the hangar.

"Damn," Hugh muttered.

She didn't let Hugh see how Rhys's words affected her. Turning her face away, she wouldn't let him see how being called a murderer tore at her. She was supposed to be all rough edges and toughness, but she was feeling very soft. Suddenly, she wanted to be alone.

"You should go after him," she said, her voice feeling hollow.

He was shaking his head. "He's just angry—he'll come around."

She went to him and put a hand on his shoulder. "You and I both know he's not headed back to your apartment."

Hugh closed his eyes, his head slumping down.

"Go get him. He can't be out there when the attack starts."

Nodding, he straightened. He seemed infinitely tired, lines suddenly creasing the underside of his eyes.

"What about the—"

"I'll ride on someone else's. Don't worry about it."

"Will you be okay?"

"Of course. One less speeder won't make a difference. We've got guns, remember? Now go."

He took a deep breath, wiped his hands, and turned to head out of the hangar too.

"Hey!"

He turned just in time to take up the gun she pressed into his chest.

"Take this," she said. "You might need it."

Hugh looked down at the gun and then at her. She opened her mouth, ready to argue with him, but this time he only nodded. Securing it in an inner pocket of his jacket, Hugh made to follow Rhys past the perimeter.

---

He could feel his skin tear as he hit the ground, but Rhys didn't slow down. Picking himself up, he was pounding down into the flatlands in a heartbeat. His pulse drummed in his ears as he made for the creek bed.

His cheeks were aflame, and his every cell was alive, vibrating with anger. He was outraged at the thought of an attack on the Charneki. His pace quickened at the resolution that they wouldn't hurt his friend. Not if he could help it.

The image of Hugh and Elena just sitting there talking about it so casually only made him angrier. How could they let it happen? How could Elena go out and shoot innocent people? She was a monster—they were both monsters if they condoned the military.

The humans were the problem, they were the antagonists. Just because they had lost their home didn't mean they could take someone else's. The idea was arrogant, and it made Rhys's blood boil. This new world was beautiful, but none of them could see it, none of them would take the time to understand. They were happy to stay behind their electric wall and rot.

He came to a skidding stop, flinging pebbles against the wall of the canyon. His chest was heaving as he looked wildly around.

"Gah!"

Ripping open his pocket, Rhys took out his reader and pressed several buttons. His face suddenly appeared on the screen.

"Zaynab, *bura galla sua*!" he said, using the Charneki phrase 'come quickly.' "Quick! I'm here!"

He swiped hurriedly and sent the video message. Once he saw that it had been received, he replaced the reader in his pocket and began to pace, praying that Zaynab remembered how to open a message.

The minutes trickled by painfully slow. His heart wouldn't stop racing, and the crunch of his boots kept sounding like gunfire.

He had to tell Zaynab what was happening, and then Zaynab had to tell the Charneki. They had to get out of there quick, or at least prepare themselves. He hoped that if they at least knew about the attack, took the element of surprise away, the coming battle would end better for them.

He took out his reader, checked to see if there was a message. Nothing. He put it back and began walking towards the encampment.

Somewhere in the back of his mind, he knew it was crazy to head to the Charneki. Zaynab never gave an indication that he had told any of the others about Rhys. Not to mention they probably wouldn't take kindly to him just waltzing into the camp.

He swallowed hard and went anyway.

The canyon wound around for a while before becoming shallower. Soon he could jump and catch the edge. Drawing himself up, he rolled onto the grass above and was quickly jogging towards the encampment. He dared not go faster, knowing the ground was littered with little canyon creek beds just like that one.

Movement up ahead made him come to a quick stop. He held perfectly still, unable to make out exactly what it was in the haze of dusk.

"Rhys?"

"Zaynab!" he called. "Over here!"

They met near a large bush, which they crouched behind.

Zaynab was out of breath, but he managed to say, "Come—quick—why?"

"I gotta tell you something."

Zaynab leaned closer, his face suddenly anxious. "There's gonna be an attack—tonight. They're gonna try and drive you out. You have to tell them—tell your sister. You have to get Zeneba away from here."

Zaynab was shaking his head, too many words coming at him all at once, but the mention of Zeneba's name made him still.

"Zeneba?"

"Yeah, you have to tell her. The humans, they are going to attack your camp. Tonight!"

"Attack?" Zaynab repeated.

Rhys made a face, frustrated that now of all times he needed to play their translation game. He took out his pocketknife without extracting the knife part and made half-hearted jabs at Zaynab.

"Attack."

"They come for us?" he asked.

"Yeah. They want to make you go away. They have big, powerful weapons, so you have to get away while—"

He stopped at the sound of something coming. They both peered over the bush to see a great figure coming straight at them, quick as a flash.

Rhys couldn't do anything before the Charneki was upon him, grabbing at his jacket and flinging him away. He hit the ground hard, kept rolling, only just stopped himself from falling down into a crevice.

His vision was swimming from the hit to his head, but he could make out a tall warrior standing protectively over Zaynab, his lipless mouth a stark line.

Rhys tried to get up, couldn't defend himself when the Charneki grabbed him up again and sent him flying.

"*Quorra! Hum murren een ua, Yaro! Quorra plia—*"

Zaynab was trying to put himself between Rhys and the warrior, trying to stop him from drawing his long sword. He couldn't, and the blade shone in the pearly moonlight as it came for Rhys.

"I don't have clearance," Hugh snapped, "but you have to let me go out there!"

"Like hell," the soldier said.

Hugh wanted to scream. He didn't know how Rhys so easily slipped past. Just standing near the perimeter, Hugh had gotten caught.

"You don't understand—my brother, he's gone out there."

The soldier paled a little. "Not possible."

"He does it all the time," Hugh persisted, "and he's gone just now. You have to let me out there—I have to get him!"

He was shaking his head. "I'm not allowed to let civilians out, it's—"

"I'm not a civilian!"

Hugh pressed a button and the surface of his gauntlet showed his credentials. The soldier glanced down at them.

"Engineers aren't military. Only military gets past this point."

"Military and little boys, apparently," he hissed.

The soldier's jaw set. "Look, there's been no perimeter breech; we would've heard it."

"I don't want to argue about the defenses. I need to find my brother."

He made to shove his way past the soldier but was quickly repelled back.

"Stand down!"

"I need to get through."

"Negative. You're not going—"

Voices came over the soldier's comlink, and from the way his face dropped, Hugh guessed it was a superior. He turned his face so that Hugh couldn't quite hear his response, but Hugh couldn't care less.

In one bound he pushed past the soldier, using his distraction, and leapt off a small rock formation, flinging himself up into a tree. His heart pumped in his ears as he climbed up as quickly as he could, the soldier shouting at him to come down. He jumped the two trees without thinking this time and scaled down just as fast.

The soldier was shouting into his comlink about a civilian jumping the perimeter, but Hugh didn't give him a second thought. Careening down out of the trees, Hugh made for the flatland.

He tried to focus on the pounding of his feet as he ran, but he couldn't stop anxious thoughts from seeping into his mind. He was terrified by what he had done—he didn't jump trees and disobey soldiers, but he cared about Rhys more than he was scared of anything. The thing was, he wasn't sure if he was more worried about or mad at Rhys.

His brother was always making trouble—Rhys *was* trouble. He wouldn't listen, wouldn't do as he was told. He couldn't understand what Hugh was trying to do, how hard Hugh was working to make sure Rhys could have a life here. Yes, it wasn't what Rhys wanted, but he was just barely twelve—he couldn't know what he wanted or what was best. If only he had let Hugh take the reins for a while, let him take care of him! It was his turn.

He tried not to kick himself while he was down, not let himself think about how royally he was failing. His turn and things were going terribly. He didn't want to admit it, but he was at a loss. He didn't know how to get through to Rhys anymore; in fact, he didn't even understand his brother anymore.

But all that didn't matter. Right then, he needed to find Rhys.

Hugh came to a stop, taking great gulps of air. He hadn't a clue where he should be going. Putting his hands on his hips, he looked about into the darkening surroundings. The early night was upon him, and the attack would start soon.

He filled his lungs to try shouting for Rhys but quickly stopped. The native encampment was somewhere to the west, but he wasn't sure how far.

Eyes widening, he pushed his sleeve up and entered a command to search for any traces of human activity. He had to point it around a bit, let it sense the air, the grass, the dirt, before he got a hit.

"Ha! Yes!"

Stooping down, he saw a small footprint creasing the short grass. The gauntlet confirmed there were traces of materials used in human boots. He lost no time following the direction of the footprint.

It led him to a small canyon, the walls almost too tall for him to pull himself out of.

"Rhys?" he whispered. The sound bounced off the walls and disappeared down the rocky crevice.

He stood silently, waiting for any noise. Slowly he squatted down and had the gauntlet run the same test again. There turned out to be a lot of human activity, the sensor picking up quite a few traces of human DNA.

"So this is where you've been," he muttered.

A scream made him jump up. His heart stopped. The sound ricocheted up and down the canyon until finally settling in amongst the dirt.

He stood shivering, unsure what to do, unable to move.

It came again, another scream, another, words in a different language, and the sound of struggling. All he could think about was Rhys, standing over him in the mouth of an alleyway, staring down a rival gang of kids. Rhys had defended him, had taken his blows. Rhys hadn't hesitated.

Squaring his jaw, Hugh made a run at the nearest canyon wall, hauled himself up when he got a fistful of grass. Bounding to his feet, he looked wildly about for the source of the noise.

He found it quickly. About a hundred yards away stood two natives, tall and glinting in the moonlight. They were bearing down on Rhys.

"NO!"

His feet moved without him having to think about it. He stumbled, nearly fell in another shallow crevice, picked himself up, went on, tripped. He was slow to get up, the wind knocked out of him, but he pushed on. Rhys's cries echoed in his head, making him go quicker, quicker.

As he got closer, his hand found its way to his jacket pocket, wrapped around the butt of the gun. He pulled it out as he ran, cocked it just like Elena had shown him.

He didn't have time to think, just filled his mind with the sight of the big native, coming at Rhys. There was a littler one beside it, its hands thrown up as if to grab Rhys. His heart stopped.

"Rhys, stay down!"

He drew the gun up, aimed.

"Hugh, wait, *no*—"

*Bang, bang!*

The natives both let out horrible screams, the bigger one collapsing down onto the little one. Rhys screamed too, made to get up, tried to get to them.

Hugh filled a hand with Rhys's collar, hauled him up, grabbed him around his chest.

Rhys struggled, still trying to get to the natives

as Hugh pulled them back, making for the cover of one of the canyons.

"C'mon! We gotta go!"

"No, no!"

One of the natives let out a howl, and Rhys writhed in his arms.

"*What have you done?*" he cried.

---

The noise was terrible as Zeneba looked down again at a battlefield, but this time there was fighting. They had come in the night like cowards, their weapons making horrible noise as they made holes in their defenses and bodies.

Several warriors, including Ondra, were swarming around her, telling her it wasn't safe, to take shelter in her tent.

She would do no such thing, though she admitted to herself how terrified she was. She watched as one of the demon's weapons struck a warrior and felt her own abdomen being ripped apart.

Her warriors rallied bravely, began sending volleys into the advancing enemy line under Chieftain Ura's direction. A few found their mark, lodging deep in those fleshy bodies, but most *clunked* off the great machines that carried a number of the demons.

Still the demons advanced, their lines unshaken by the Charneki's attempts.

"We must dig in," she said. Addressing the nearest warrior, she directed, "Draw in our lines to the crest of this hill—it'll be more defensible." She put a hand on Ondra's shoulder. "Tell the Chieftain to withdraw to our line when he can no longer hold."

"I'm not going to leave you," he said, his eyes as fierce as an *igla*'s.

"That's an order, Ondra," she said.

He held her gaze for a long moment before finally running off with the other warrior, both having their tasks. Another warrior from the Guard came to replace them.

She watched anxiously, her innards feeling as if they were tied in knots, as their lines closed in around her, making a semi-circle around the crest of the hill. Chieftain Ura and his men remained a salient point, engaged most heavily with the demons.

For a few moments, it seemed like they had routed the demons. Warriors on *garans* arrived at the front lines. They put their great shields down to protect them and the *garans'* heads and advanced past the line, pushing forward. Some of the enemy shots glanced off the shields and shells.

One *garan* fell at a shot to the leg, its foot blown clean off. The warrior tumbled down, rolled on the ground, found his footing. He almost made it to the demon line, his sword gleaming in the moonlight. It took ten of their shots to bring him down.

The *garan* line broke. The creatures cried out in

pain, harmonizing with the warriors' battle cries as they jumped from their laboring mounts, making a run for the enemy. A few punched through, sweeping long swords and spears over the smaller demons and punishing them for their cowardly attack.

This didn't stop the demons long. When all the warriors lay dead, they advanced again.

Zeneba stood cold and still, her hands trembling. It felt like there was a rock lodged in her throat and a dagger in her gut. Words, thoughts escaped her. A tear slipped out of her eye. What was she to do? What could any of them do?

Ondra was suddenly in front of her, shouting something. It took a moment for her eyes to focus on him, and by the time she heard what he said, he was shaking her shoulders.

"Zeneba, *please*," he said, his eyes wild, "you must go!"

She found herself shaking her head. "I'm needed here."

"You're needed alive! They're breaking through—we can't stop them. Please, please, you must go. We'll cover your retreat."

She took another look at the coming demons and felt her courage slipping. She almost collapsed under the weight of her mistake. They should not have come. She should not have presumed to make them see reason.

Ondra wasted no more time and began urging her towards the southern slope. Other warriors raced ahead to ready the *garans*.

"No," she said, "wait."

"Zeneba, we must get you out of here!"

"Zaynab," she murmured. "Where's Zaynab? I can't leave without him."

"I'll find him," he promised, "but, please, you have to go. I'll catch up with him."

"No, I won't—" But he was gone.

She stood there unmoving, feeling completely detached from her body.

Someone crying out, "Golden One!" wrenched

her back into place. She turned to find Yaro coming quickly to her. His face scared her more than anything else ever had. She opened her mouth to ask him what was going on when he collapsed onto his knees before her and held out his arms.

She sank down too at the sight.

"No . . . "

With trembling hands she touched the still, bloody body in Yaro's arms.

"*No!* Zaynab, no!"

She pulled him to her, wrapped her arms around him, cradled him, rocked back and forth, her face contorting. She turned her face up to the cold, dark sky and let out a cry as her soul threatened to tear apart.

Yaro tried to explain what had happened, but he couldn't form anything more than a word. He couldn't take his glassy eyes off Zaynab.

"It . . . it . . . k-killed . . . " he said.

But Zeneba could barely hear him. All she could do was clutch at her brother.

From behind, Ondra came upon them.

"I couldn't find—" He caught sight of Zaynab. "No . . ."

Her tears splashed down onto Zaynab's face as she continued rocking back and forth, back and forth, all her muscles clenched and on fire.

"Zeneba . . ."

She stilled, her breath catching. She looked down.

Zaynab's eyes were small slits, barely open, but he looked up at her. He was trying to reach up.

She took his hand, crushed it against her.

"H-hold on," she said, "I'll see to you. Y-you're going to be . . . " She could say no more, her words lost to tears and tremors.

Zaynab shook his head once; it was all he could manage.

"Don't . . . don't be . . . mad," he murmured, "at me."

"I'm not, I'm not!" she said. "I just want you to stay with me. That's all I want."

"I'll stay with you," he said, "even if my body can't."

"No," she sobbed, "no, all of you will stay with me. You'll see—we'll . . . we'll . . ."

She looked about at the warriors gathered around them. Their skin was all steeped blue in sorrow. None of them could do anything.

"Find me a healer!" she snapped.

"Zeneba, they're not all bad," Zaynab murmured.

"What?" She pulled him up closer.

"The demons—they're not all . . ."

"But they d-did this to you," she said, her voice cracking.

"Not all . . . demons," he repeated, his mouth beginning to slacken, his eyes fading.

"No, no! Zaynab, no, don't leave me!"

He grinned. "Never," he said.

He went still in her arms.

She sat with her mouth agape, her hands trembling, as she watched his skin darken until it was black. Letting out a wail, she put her head against his, wrapped her whole body around him.

Elder Vasya came too late. His healing powers were useless.

Her sobs drowned out the sound of the fighting just over the other side of the hill. Nothing mattered. She was numb to everything but the knife stuck right in her heart. She would not be moved, no matter how they pleaded, would only lie there, clutching him to her, feeling the life-warmth seep out of him.

Finally even Yaro had collected enough of his wits to urge her to get to her *garan*.

"We must make for Karak," he said, his voice hollow.

"Go," she said, "leave me. I stay with him."

"Please, Zeneba, we must get you—"

"*I said go!*"

Yaro shouted orders at the other Guards, called for her *garan* to be brought.

"I'll not leave him!"

She sensed Ondra over her, felt his arms come around her. She tried to stop him, but her limbs were too heavy to move.

He picked both her and Zaynab up and bore them quickly to the awaiting *garan*. Once they were on, he jumped up behind her, took the reins in his hands, and called for the retreat.

The *garans* made southeast as quickly as they could, the rest of the outfit bringing up the rear. The demons' weapons rang out with horrible echoes in the dark night.

Ondra pulled her closer when he felt her begin to tremble. She convulsed with sobs, though she hadn't any tears left.

He opened his mouth to try and soothe her.

"Don't."

He closed his eyes and grimaced.

The rhythmic pounding of the lumbering *garans* lulled her into numbness again. Her eyes were glazed as she stared out at the riders beside her. She spotted Elder Vasya riding a mount next to them.

Her lips spread out over her teeth in a sneer as she looked upon him. Her heart began to beat again, her blood running molten where it had been ice a moment ago.

"Are you happy now, Elder? Are you pleased?" she hissed.

Elder Vasya's eyes widened in horror as Zeneba's narrowed, her skin rippling into a wrathful red.

"You have your war."